SHOW JUMPING TEAM

BY

CLARE O'BEARA

ISBN: 978-1-910544-05-1

Cover photograph © Clare O'Beara.

The subjects of the photograph have no connection to this story or characters.

Cover art: Allan Tennent.

Published by Clare O'Beara

Show Jumping Team

Madeline is sixteen with nothing to do in the school holidays. The rural Irish town is quiet and shops are not hiring part-time staff. To keep her out of trouble she is encouraged to join a Riding Club and learn to compete. Her borrowed horse Moonrock has plenty of experience.

The same can't be said for Alabama, the young chestnut mare purchased by Karen's moneyed parents. Karen is expected to succeed, even though other club members - such as Niall, a farmer boy - resent the fact that her father bought up farmland for building. Karen's only ally is Jen who works at the livery yard, training young horses.

Can the young adults put aside their differences and learn to be a team - when it really matters?

Titles by Clare O'Beara

Dystopian Science Fiction

Dining Out Around The Solar System

Dining Out With The Ice Giants

Dining Out With The Gas Giants

Crime

Murder at Irish Mensa

Murder at Scottish Mensa

Murder at Dublin Mensa

Murder at Kildare Mensa

Murder at Wicklow Mensa

Romantic Suspense

Silks And Sins

Young Adult

Show Jumping Team

Rodeo Finn

Short Story

The Prisoner in The Tower

Anthologies

Dreamless Roads

A Pint And A Haircut

Author's Website:

http://www.clareobeara.ie

Reviews of Clare's books

Murder At Irish Mensa

It is always refreshing---like with Miss Marple---when a non-detective solves a crime. Especially when the official detectives are a bit overbearing. Murder at Irish Mensa is one such case... Can brains do what police procedure cannot?
Read this unusual tale of a tree surgeon working sleuthing between energy spent looking for a new house and tending her duties as organiser [US: organizer] of the meeting to find the answer. You'll enjoy the ride.
Larry Winebrenner, author of The Henri Derringer Mysteries

This book had everything I like: cats; an unusual, feisty female; a (subtle) romantic element; an interesting set of problems; a modicum of esoteric knowledge; gentle humour; and a realistic characterisation of the sorts of people I tend to hang out with myself.... It was the perfect weekend relaxation.
Francesca on Amazon

Murder at Dublin Mensa

The third Mensa mystery lives up to the first two.... The story is equally exciting and centres on the same three principal characters. Read it!
Francesca on Amazon

Dining Out Around The Solar System

There's lots of pleasant surprises in store for you in this thoughtful, at times ultra-cynical, fantasy excursion into the not so very far into the future dystopian society of the UK and Eire....
One plus of Earth's industrial exploration of the planetary system is that sentient life has been found on the other seven planets (and titchy Pluto), and guess what? They all have marketable resources, including migrant labour. And all of them want in on Terra's solo mastery of interplanetary travel....

This is high concept fantasy that does science in an holistic and well-researched manner that takes you to unexpected places in the human spirit, whether that resides in the breast of a native of London, or Dublin, or Mercury, or Mars, or Saturn. For good or ill. Well-written and observed, Clare O'Beara brings her considerable experience as a journalist to bear in conjuring a totally believable future multicultural society with bells (and knobs) on....

The rewards are all threaded through the whole and, most definitely, there in the ending. Highly recommended for all those who don't need ray guns (or any guns much) at regular intervals in their intellectual fantasy thrillers.

Jan Hawke, Owner and CEO DreamWorlds Publishing

The plot actually follows the paths of these two journalists from their education and as they develop their careers. It leads to some thrilling story-lines as we follow some of the main stories they cover. The two main characters, Donal and Myron are very endearing and they have a close bond and friendship that is rare in any time!... I enjoyed the human aspects in this book and really enjoyed when the journalists dipped into history....

I would recommend this book to Science Fiction fans but also to people who enjoy stories based around a strong friendship where a bond is so great they would sacrifice anything and everything for the other.

Roisin Bisland on Amazon

Rodeo Finn

Rodeo Finn by Clare O'Beara is a beautifully written book. I enjoy a book that is both a good story and educational at the same time. If you have a young teen who loves reading books about horses and would like to learn more about them, this is a great book to read. It is clean with many lessons of life. I appreciate the way Finn was a responsible, helpful, respectful young lady.

Melanie Bennet, Author of Learning To Dance In The Rain

Dining Out With The Ice Giants

Dining Out With The Ice Giants is a gem of a book that creates a world that feels just like ours – but for the several species of Aliens who have immigrated in search of employment. These alien immigrants end up filling the marginal roles that poor immigrants fill in real world society. Suitably, the aliens' willingness to work for low pay elicits resentment and scorn from Earth citizens. Moreover, scoundrels both human and alien find ways to manipulate and exploit the most powerless among the aliens.

Donal and his best buddy Myron are unofficial human ambassadors to the resident alien communities in London... This book is highly enjoyable, thought provoking, and definitely worth reading.

Alexis Grove, Author of The Aeon Trilogy

With this second helping in the Dining Out science fantasy series, we're filling in some of the gaps in Donal and Myron's journalistic career and finding more quirky insights into the secret lives of the visitors from the outermost planets in the System. The Ice Giants are, of course, Uranus and Neptune, but immigrants from dwarf planet Pluto are also prominent in this book where we find out more about their early days in London before they go into the ice cream and frosty treats trade.

What I really like about O'Beara's dystopian London are the left field details that take what's starting to happen in the present to logical but often surprising and illuminating conclusions as hinted at in headlines of the book blurb.

Yet another excellent and insightful read from Clare O'Beara, and, I hope, not the last we'll see of Donal and Myron.

Jan Hawke, Owner and CEO DreamWorlds Publishing

Show Jumping Team
Contents

Chapter Fifteen

Chapter Sixteen

Author's Note on Language

This book is written in British English, so readers used to American English may find some spellings unfamiliar.
Examples:
organise for organize;
colour for color;
theatre for theater.

While the details were correct when this book was written, some items such as regulations may be subject to change.

SHOW JUMPING TEAM

CHAPTER ONE

"Ghost estate," said Janey Coughlan, kicking a chunk of rubble as she sauntered down the unfinished concrete path towards half-built houses. Weeds grew up through cracks. "Sounds scary doesn't it? Really cool. Like the zombie banks that lent the money to build these useless houses."

"Not scary," said Madeline, hands in her jeans pockets. She wanted to say, depressing, but knew that Janey would laugh at her. "Just – sad, you know? This used to be a field, maybe ponies grazed here or the farmer took in crops. And now there's three houses occupied, it looks like, out of twenty."

"Ponies are for little kids. Who'd want to come and live in this pathetic town anyway. Nothing ever happens here. I wish I lived in Dublin." Janey stopped and sat on a milk crate next to a front door without a number; the cable for the porch light hung emptily above her head and there was no doorbell, just a wire. She took out a cigarette pack from her jacket pocket. "Want one?"

"I don't smoke," said Madeline automatically.

"It's not real cigarettes, it's the fun stuff. Try it."

Madeline squatted on her heels as Janey lit a home-made cigarette and sucked in the smoke. She didn't want to try the stuff. She didn't want to be here, doing nothing. But what else was there to do?

"Madeline, I am so disappointed in you," exclaimed the girl's mother. Madeline avoided her eyes as she closed the passenger door of her uncle's car and walked into the house.

"Thank you for bringing her home, John," she heard behind her. Then the door closed and the girl turned to face her parent. Like her mother she had dark hair which tended to waves, and blue eyes.

"It was just the once, Mum. I'm sixteen for goodness' sake, that stuff has been around town for years and I never tried it before. I won't again either, I didn't like it."

"I never knew there was cannabis in town. You should have told the Guards. No evenings out for you from now on. And that brassie Janey Coughlan comes nowhere near this house in future, and you're to stay away from her."

"Fine. I don't like her much anyway."

"Then why were you hanging around with her?"

"There's nothing else to do." Nothing much if you lived in an Irish country town that wasn't on the tourist maps. None of the shops had jobs going. All her school friends were away for the summer, visiting relatives who'd emigrated, and the farm kids were kept busy on the land, plus they were dull as ditchwater.

"I'll find you something to do. Try weeding the garden."

Madeline hesitated, just long enough to see the expression on her mother's face harden.

"I'm getting into my old jeans then," she said, turning and heading upstairs.

Eamonn, Madeline's little brother, was sitting on the top step, hidden by the turn.

"You really took drugs?" he asked wide-eyed. "What's it like?"

The girl half-wanted to impress him. How pathetic would that be, she scorned herself immediately.

"Not great, actually. The smoke tasted bad and it made me feel sick. Then I did get sick. That's why Uncle John stopped – he thought I was ill."

"So you don't recommend it then," he said, disappointed.

"I wouldn't waste your pocket money." Madeline trudged on to get changed, already picking the music she'd listen to while weeding, thinking that if nothing else she'd learnt the lesson of not doing anything dodgy where passers-by could see.

That evening of course Madeline's father had to be told. He listened in silence, with the sound on the television turned off.

"Have you learnt anything?" he asked his daughter.

"Yes dad."

"Will you do it again?"

"No dad."

"All right then," Mr Kelly said. "Just remember that whatever you do now, can follow you around all your life. So don't get into trouble with the law and don't write about this on your social network pages, or anything. In two years' time you'll have finished school and be looking for a job or college place. Employers do net searches."

"She says she has nothing else to do," Mrs Kelly stated.

"Not since the riding school closed down," agreed Madeline. She was relieved that her dad was being so reasonable. She hadn't got into such serious trouble since she was a kid, but at her age, they couldn't send her to her room or stop her pocket money.

"Well, find something." He handed a local newspaper over to the girl. "Something within cycling distance."

'Rider/ groom wanted for sensible cob. Stabled with owner. Ideal for Riding Club activities. Reply Box No. 14.'

Madeline read the small ad twice. She thought of asking her mother if it was okay to reply. Then she shook her head, thinking that her father had told her to find something. She typed up a reply on the laptop and printed it off; she'd given her name, address, age and riding experience. As an afterthought she'd added that when the riding school closed, she'd written to Riding For The Disabled offering to help with lessons, but had been told that as the pupils go to special schools the lessons aren't given during school holidays. She had to give her home phone number, because her mum had confiscated her phone to stop her chatting to Janey Coughlan. She posted the letter, not expecting a result. The summer holidays would be long and bleak without horses.

Niall eased the reins to let his dun pony catch his breath while he memorised the course. Right – let's go, he thought, and the pony moved into a canter without hesitation, ears pricked and keen.

"Niall Johnson and Tigger next to jump."

The bell rang as he saluted the judges and he took a steady approach to the first fence, a simple spread of poles and straw bales. The dun bucked as he jumped and the boy held on with his knees. Fence two, a vertical – right turn to three, a gate – straight on to a stile, left turn to a wall, steady before a double of straight to spread, finish with a good stretch over a triple bar. The cheers rose – then faded, and Niall was alone with his sweating pony. The rusty barrels supporting plain poles disapproved of his daydream, but he didn't care, and a prancing Tigger cared even less.

Shay Broughton unsaddled his horse and rubbed him down, then carried the tack to the box of his new arrival. The young horse wagged its ears suspiciously and snorted at the saddle. Shay groomed the youngster lightly before tacking it with the snaffle bridle and old saddle. He tugged down the peak of his cloth cap and led the young horse out of the stable, unshod hoofs soft on the concrete of his yard.

"Jen," he called to his stable girl, "would you hold him while I mount?" The blonde girl, her sweater sleeves rolled up and her jeans stained, set down the handles of her barrow and came to help.

"He nearly kicked me while I was cleaning his stable," she informed her employer. "Got between me and the door and showed me his heels."

"Obviously thought you were threatening him with the fork," returned Shay calmly, checking his girth. "Don't forget, he hasn't been handled much. Next time tie him up."

"Next time," retorted Jen, holding his reins and offside stirrup as the man mounted, "I'll do his box when he's outside."

"Then how will he learn stable manners?"

"Be careful with him – I do wish you'd wear a hard hat on youngsters."

"Nonsense," Shay dismissed the notion. "Forty years I've been riding, forty years, Jen." He rode quietly to the schooling field and proceeded to school the brown gelding. The horse, a strapping half-bred with a strong neck and plenty of leg bone, mouthed his snaffle awkwardly and either poked his nose or hollowed his back, but Shay knew that time would improve him. There was plenty of time.

"Karen dear, welcome home."

"Hello Mum. The bus was crowded as usual. How are you and Dad?"

"I'm fine, just organising a bridge party for this evening. Your father's in London for a conference.

How was term? I'm sure the exams were no problem to you."

"Went okay I think – school was fun. But I'm looking forward to riding Merry again. Do you need me to make up a four? I'd rather just hand around the sandwiches, I haven't played since Easter."

Mrs Langourne laughed forgivingly, smoothing a crease in her silk dress.

"I should have enough numbers, all people you know. I'm sure they'll be delighted to see what a lovely young lady you've turned out to be. Do wear a pretty dress, dear, they'll be here at eight. Would you like some tea first? And you ought to run down to the stables. There's a wonderful surprise for you."

Karen looked askance at her mother. They both had red hair – auburn, her mother described her darker shade, but Karen's was orange as carrots. One such surprise years ago had been the news that she was being sent to boarding school. Another had been her enrolment in the Pitch and Putt club, a game which Karen played as infrequently as possible. What could her mother possibly have done at the stables?

"A new saddle for Merry?" she wondered.

"Not in your good clothes, dear. The smell of horses does so stick to them."

Karen went to her room at the far end of their extensive bungalow, changed into jeans, shirt and sweatshirt with trainers, and trotted down the drive, across the road, through the fence and over three fields to Shay Broughton's livery yard.

"Mum," Karen asked when she returned, "where is Merry? There was a big chestnut mare in her box and the yard girl said you'd bought her. Mr Broughton was busy schooling."

"We sold Merry," trilled her mother. "You'd grown out of her, you're too old for ponies now, you're sixteen after all."

"I'm not too old for a fourteen-two. Where did she go?"

"Oh, Mr Broughton found her a good home. A nice trekking centre, he said they take good care of their ponies and he recommends it to people. So she'll be out and about on the hills all summer, won't she have fun? But he had a really top-class young horse, a chance too good to miss, she has jumping pedigree and a Thoroughbred mother or grandmother or something. Just what you need."

"She's huge," gasped Karen. "Sixteen-two, the yard girl said. And only five. I'll never manage her."

"Of course you will, you're an excellent rider. We were so proud of you when you won those Pony Club rosettes and that shield."

"That mare's too big for Pony Club," protested Karen.

"Exactly," said her mother, beaming. "So we've enrolled you in the local Riding Club. The adult version. You will enjoy it."

CHAPTER TWO

Madeline put down the phone and wandered into the kitchen. Her mother was peeling potatoes and her brother sat playing computer games with one of his friends.

"Pat," said Eamonn over the Gameboy noises, "this is my sister. She's Mad." He always got that in, it had ceased to annoy her.

"How come?" wondered the friend.

"Mad by name, mad by nature." The pair of them laughed.

"Was that phone call for me?" asked Mrs Kelly.

"No, for me."

"Oh, she's got a boyfriend!" crowed Eamonn.

"I do not."

"Leave her alone, Eamonn," insisted Mrs Kelly. "What's up, Madeline?"

"I answered an ad looking for someone to take care of a horse. The owner says can I come over today."

"Oh. Who is it?"

"He says he's Gary Mitchell. It's his sister's horse but she'll be away all summer."

"Mitchells, I don't know them but I've heard your aunt talk about them. Respectable people. All right then – can you get there on your bike?"

"Yes, I've got directions."

"Make sure you look tidy."

"Better take off that Guns 'N' Roses t-shirt," giggled Eamonn. "Proves you're mad."

"You don't appreciate good music," retorted the girl. All the same, she did change the shirt, just in case.

Gary Mitchell smiled at the dark-haired, slim teenager and introduced himself.

"I'm a teacher," he explained, "so I have long holidays like you." He began to lead the way to the stable and paddock at the side of his comfortable old family home. "I'm getting married later this year but for now I'm at a loose end." Their feet tapped on the concrete around the stable. A grey cob's chunky head and big kind eyes appeared over the half-door. "This is old Moonrock. He taught me to ride, then my sister. She had him while I was at college, but this summer she's away with friends in France, picking fruit."

"He's beautiful," gasped Madeline, unsure how to address a teacher out of school. She offered her hand to the grey, who sniffed her thoroughly and began to lick her palm.

"Oh, he's a good old sort. I'm too big for him now and I'm not going to put the work in for competition, so there's nobody else to ride him. Moonrock was fed up doing nothing, and fat as butter from grazing, so I brought him in and started lungeing him and put that ad in the paper. If you suit him, I'll supervise as needed and drive you to shows. Like to ride him?"

Madeline had never ridden anything higher than fourteen-two, and Moonrock was a hand higher, and solidly built. His head had become almost white with age, but there was a sparkle in his dark eyes.

"I'd love to."

Gary – Madeline soon forgot that he was a teacher – fetched the tack and they tacked up the horse. A snaffle bridle, a martingale and a general purpose saddle with string girth. Madeline didn't admit that she had never used a running martingale. She noticed that the tack badly needed soaping, but thought mentioning it might be rude. Moonrock stood still while his rider mounted. She was wearing a borrowed hard hat. She picked up the reins and the cob moved off obediently. He wasn't so lively as she had feared and if he was a shade slow to answer the bit, at least he didn't take much stopping. The paddock sloped and he made heavy weather of climbing the hill.

"He's not fit," apologised Gary. "Too much grass and too little work."

"It's hard to be fit as a fiddle if you're built like a double bass," said Madeline, and they both laughed.

"After a couple of weeks' work he'll be ready for competition with you. If you'd like."

"I'm game," agreed Madeline.

Karen, her long red hair tied into a sensible ponytail, stood with her hands in her pockets, sizing up the new mare.

"Like her?" asked Shay cheerily as he hosed wet mud off a horse's legs.

"Yes," said Karen, because there was nothing else to say.

"Name's Alabama. She's broken, riding, nicely schooled and ready to go on." He turned off the hose and led the horse into a stable to dry off its legs. Karen stood looking at Alabama and seeing only Merry, a Connemara pony. She had found that trekking centre and seen that Merry was well cared for and busy. The pony would work all summer but would rest during winter; she would be well fed and every tourist who could afford it would bounce up and down hill paths on her uncomplaining back.

"Perhaps you'd like to trek on her yourself sometime?" the new owners had invited.

Alabama showed her teeth in a horsey yawn. Her back seemed far up in the air and her neck as long as a giraffe's. Didn't people say that chestnut mares were giddy? Or hot-tempered? Karen wasn't sure where she'd start to tack her or even what bridle to use. A long thin blaze ran the length of the mare's face, petering out at her muzzle. Her large ears flickered sharply to a figure coming around the corner of the stable block.

"Hello Karen," said Jen with a smile. "Come to try her? She's very green but has a lovely temperament."

"Okay," said the girl with a shrug. "Would you tack her for me?"

Jen suppressed her inclination to frown. Typical of the wealthy family, she thought. They expected everyone else to do their work. One didn't upset good customers like the Langournes so she went to fetch correctly-fitting tack.

Karen fastened the strap of her riding cap and accepted a leg-up from Jen, who held the reins until she was sure that Karen had found her stirrups and sorted out her reins.

"Better take it easy if you haven't ridden all term," she advised.

"I will," agreed Karen, "I'll just get used to her. She's a long way off the ground."

"Take her out to the schooling field."

Jen had work to do; work never finished in a livery and dealing yard. Most hunters were turned out now but summer brought young horses to school and children's ponies. These often had to be taught everything from picking up their feet for the farrier, to loading into a trailer. When they had absorbed basic lessons they had to learn to be calm while music played and plastic bags flapped on strings. Parents wanted unshockable ponies for their kids.

Karen had been rather hoping that the blonde girl would come along, in case the mare did anything dangerous, but she set her teeth and walked Alabama out to the field. Each stride covered a lot of ground. When she tried to rein in and tighten the girth, the fresh mare fidgeted and refused to stand still. She chewed the bit and tossed her head right up and down, pulling the smooth leather reins through Karen's hands. The girl regained her hold and the mare sidled crabwise, keen to go.

"Walk on then. Merry never did that. Why can't you be sensible?" Five-year-olds, she knew, were anything but sensible. She took the mare to a corner formed by hedges and managed to trot in passable circles and figures of eight. Alabama still chewed noisily and Karen didn't know whether this was good or bad. Once she tried to lean down and check the girth but Alabama got excited and broke into a long canter stride, so she had her hands full just staying aboard. She steered in circles determinedly and soon felt the chestnut relax into a smooth pace. She would take some getting used to, but it was going to be fun being so high up, able to look right down on ponies.

Karen felt something slipping. She clapped her legs tight in alarm and grabbed the mane. Alabama took exception to such treatment and gave a small buck. The saddle slipped and Karen screamed. She felt herself falling as the mare bucked at the moving saddle. The ground met her hard and fast, knocking away her breath for a few seconds. When she managed to get to her feet it was to see Alabama galloping madly back to the yard, saddle hanging under her tender stifle and stirrup irons banging her legs.

Shay had to spend ten minutes with the terrified mare before he could remove the saddle.

"Hey, Niall," called a voice and the boy turned as he came out of the library. "Haven't seen you since school ended. What're you up to?"

"Keeping busy," Niall assured his friend. "Working on the farm and running errands."

"We're going for a bike ride on Sunday, three of us, taking a picnic. D'you want to come?"

"Thanks, but I'll be busy – doing another sort of riding."

"Why did I bother asking?" The lad grinned. "Got a show?"

"That's right," said Niall. "Riding club. I'm doing well in the League and the team selectors will be watching."

Madeline rode Moonrock every day, getting him fit and rewarding his efforts with apples. She developed stronger legs from keeping him up to his bridle, as Gary insisted; sometimes Gary would lunge the grey with Madeline riding with no reins. After a few days Gary let her trot over poles and jumps a foot high; after a week the jumps gradually rose to two foot six with a three foot spread.

"That's high enough for Primary," he told her. "Riding Clubs grade each rider and Primary is, as the name would suggest, the first grade. You've never competed so you start at the simplest level. I'm a non-riding member of Dore Hill Riding Club so I can propose you as a member."

"I've jumped three foot six on ponies," Madeline assured him. Gary seemed to be enjoying himself.

"The Regional Team Challenge will be a big day for all the clubs at the end of summer. Have you got proper riding clothes?"

"I've got beige jodhpurs and a white shirt. Will my school tie do?"

"Sure. I can lend you a white tie for Inter-Club shows. No jacket? Don't worry, I'll give you the one I wore as a wee slip of a lad."

"I am looking forward to the shows, but I'm a bit nervous too," Madeline confessed. "I've never done anything like this."

"Most people are nervous to start," Gary assured her. "You'll get used to it. And you'll have a great time. So will old Moonrock, he loves a day out."

Karen rode Alabama every day, with, on Shay's advice, a breastplate saddle check which held the saddle forward. The mare was too light of muscle behind the saddle and too narrow in the ribs, being young, he explained. Until she had strengthened up some more, the check would stop her saddle from slipping. Provided of course that her girth was tight. One day when Shay was schooling his young gelding over small jumps Karen followed suit with Alabama, mainly because she was bored with flatwork. She was pleasantly surprised by the way that the mare picked up her feet over the trotting poles and bounced over the cross-pole, then cantered on purposefully to a small spread.

"Got a lovely pop, hasn't she?" Shay called. Karen nodded, flushed with pleasure. Shay laid out a small course and told her about strides and collection. Ponies were good at sorting themselves out, he said, their legs were so short that they could usually put in an extra stride or take off from under the fence if necessary. But horses were different. Their legs and strides were longer and they naturally carried more weight on their forehands, making it difficult for them to lift off the ground.

"Ponies are smart about getting out of trouble too," he summarised, "horses have to be taught. Your mare has jumping blood and she's had good early lessons. See what she'll do over that course – just steer straight and don't let her rush."

Karen got around the course using a lot of leg when the mare eyed a new obstacle with suspicion. She returned to the double and made a better job of it second time.

"She's great. Cleared it by miles," she declared, patting the chestnut.

"She's registered you know," said Shay. "For proper jumping. So are you, your mother asked me to see to it."

"SJAI?" asked Karen doubtfully. That sounded like big league. "I thought I was going to Riding Clubs this summer."

"I do both," said Shy with a shrug. "Come to think of it, there's a fixture clash this weekend. I'm going to Dore Hill and Jen will try the black mare at showing. You could do either."

Karen found the schedules and noted a Show Hunter class for four- and five-year-old horses. Snaffle bridle permitted, so she wouldn't have to worry about a complicated double bridle. This class was being held at a registered show, where she could watch the jumping. Karen decided that this sounded like an easy option. Less chance to make a fool of herself.

CHAPTER THREE

Madeline led Moonrock into the single horsebox trailer and Gary raised the ramp.

"He hasn't been out for ages," said the horse's owner. "He's looking forward to it." Indeed the grey had a jaunty air as he loaded, and now he nudged Madeline's hand expectantly. "Carrot for him," prompted Gary. "He always gets one in the horsebox as a treat."

The girl joined Gary in the old four-wheel drive and they moved off gently with the trailer in tow.

"It's important to go easy with horses," he said. "A young or nervous horse could fall if I cornered fast or braked sharply. Moonrock stands foursquare like an old sailor."

Madeline nodded, looking at the tack on the back seat. The show had been her excuse to clean and soap every item thoroughly, and the dark leather gleamed and stirrups shone. Her mount had required a good grooming too, since being so pale his coat showed any stains. She'd washed his tail in a bucket, which had bothered him not at all, and was rewarded by a snow-white tail today. She'd been relieved to hear that plaits were not expected, since she'd never plaited. Gary didn't seem to have either, though he said his sister had been more fussy about appearance. Nerves had caused Madeline to miss her breakfast, yet she wasn't at all hungry as they arrived at the show field at eleven o'clock.

"Oh, I see jumps!" she exclaimed, pointing across the field to a set of poles and wings being assembled. Gary grinned at her excitement as he parked in a line of similar vehicles.

"It's polite to offer to help with course-building," he hinted.

"But I don't know anyone – or how to put up fences."

"Come on." Gary glanced in the door of the trailer to check Moonrock before leading her over to the other members. One or two people were dressed for riding, but anyone lifting poles or barrels wore jeans. He introduced the girl to a lady called Maeve Conroy, who was club secretary.

"Delighted to welcome you to Dore Hill, Madeline," said Maeve, beaming. "I don't ride but my two children do. I have a membership card here for you." The joining fee and entries were being paid by the girl's father, who reckoned that this still saved money compared with twice-weekly riding lessons.

Gary introduced Madeline to the course builders and she was allotted the task of distributing cups to the fences; the metal or plastic cups fixed to each fence wing to support the poles. Madeline thought that she was doing fine, until a man pointed out to her that he was building a plank fence.

"Oh," she said, looking at the striped planks. "That's right." She took her cups away and asked Gary quietly what she'd done wrong.

"Doesn't that kind need cups?"

"Yes," he said, chuckling, "but flat ones. A plank wouldn't fall out of those round cups if a horse hit it. Look in the box for flat-topped ones." Feeling like a real novice, Madeline corrected her mistake. She walked the finished course with Gary when the numbers were set in place; as she'd been assured the fences were no more than a hop for Moonrock, so she would be able to concentrate on finding her way. A few new arrivals were walking the course as they unloaded Moonrock and tacked him. Madeline suddenly felt so nervous that she was certain she would forget the nine-fence course. She kept repeating it in her mind.

"I'll walk him around while you change," offered Gary. "You can change in the horsebox; most people do."

Niall arrived already dressed in riding clothes, since he hacked to shows on Tigger. He dismounted and tied the well-trained pony to a fencepost, using a halter and leadrope, while he walked the course and said good-day to everyone. Then he made his entry and returned to Tigger, remounting. He spotted the Mitchells' trailer; there was Gary and Moonrock. He nudged Tigger over in that direction, leaning down to adjust his girths.

"Hi Caroline," he greeted the girl on Moonrock, and was puzzled when she did not reply. He looked up and shock struck him; a strange girl was regarding him from Moonrock's back. "Oh, you're not Caroline – sorry!"

"Madeline Kelly," she told him.

"New member? I'm Niall Johnson. What grade are you riding?"

"Primary."

"I'm Advanced Intermediate."

"That sounds complicated.

"Means I get to go against the clock. You won't. How come you're riding Moonrock?"

"Gary's sister is away," said Madeline. She didn't want to say that she'd answered an advert. Niall must go to a different school, she was thinking, and if she wasn't mistaken he was one of those boring farm lads. Pity, because he had nice blue eyes, and a strong set of shoulders. Must be from hauling all that hay.

Madeline had forgotten her course, and nearly panicked when the loudspeaker crackled into life. The practice arena was near the jumping arena, and she was able to pick out the fences as she trotted around the grassy area. Gary put the practice fence to an X and directed the girl to keep out of everyone's way, take her turn jumping and jump with the red flag on the right. This ensured that the jump would only be taken from one direction, for safety. Moonrock was happy and willing, and jumped with aplomb.

An older man on a big brown horse tackled the practice jump and rode into the competition arena. The announcer said,

"Primary competition. First to go, Shay Broughton on Cootehill Lad. Hors concours." A bell rang and the man rode around the course at a steady pace, meeting every fence well and clearing them. Everyone wore crash helmets and long riding boots; Madeline's were made of rubber.

When Madeline's turn arrived she trotted into the arena and paused for the bell. "Madeline Kelly on Moonrocket," came the voice. She waited. Just when she thought she'd missed the bell, it did ring, and she wasn't sure if she should have saluted. Setting her jaw, she kicked the cob into a canter and pointed him at the first fence. He cleared the small spread and Madeline guided him to the second fence, the planks then the double. After this two fences presented themselves and the girl froze. Which one? Blue or red? What number had the double been? Left or right? The cob, receiving no clear signal, faltered. Making up her mind, Madeline pushed for the right-hand fence, but Moonrock couldn't take off and stopped, throwing up his head in protest. The girl, blushing with embarrassment, turned and rode in a circle, presenting her mount properly at the fence. Moonrock kicked up his heels to show that it hadn't been his fault. They finished the round without further mishap.

"Three faults," declared the voice as the pair left the arena.

"Oh, I am sorry, I forgot," Madeline told Gary, ashamed.

"Not to worry, you'll get it next time," said the man with a shrug. There were other competitors.

"I must have looked very novicey compared to that first rider," sighed the girl, patting her horse.

"Shay?" Gary looked surprised. "He's not your grade. He's schooling a young horse, that's all. When you hear hors concours, that means not in the competition."

The other two riders were clear and the judges invited everyone to jump again, so Madeline got a second chance and made a much better effort this time, One rider had a clear round and one had four faults, and Madeline went clear; this made her third. Maeve Conroy presented the rosettes; red for first, blue for second, yellow for third. They cantered happily around the arena, where the course builders were occupied with raising each fence for the next class.

Moonrock was rewarded with a carrot and, tack removed, he was allowed to graze in a headcollar while he cooled.

"Why did the judge call him Moonrocket?" Madeline asked Gary.

"That's his name. He was dark grey as a young horse, with a blonde tail. I just liked the name Moonrocket." He paused to consider. "I guess he was a bit livelier then."

Madeline had been given back her phone, as her mother considered that horses might cause emergencies. She sent a brief text home to say that her class was over but she hadn't won anything, then turned off the phone because everyone found ringing phones annoying.

Shay Broughton came over to talk to them, similarly leading his young horse. He had removed his helmet and Madeline now discovered that the man was completely bald on top, with hair just around the edges, like a monk's head.

Niall competed in the Intermediate class. After two rounds the three Intermediate riders shared first place while the Advanced Intermediates went on to jump against the clock. Niall memorised a short course and drawn second, had the advantage of watching his opponent. Tigger knew the routine and bucked excitedly as he began his round. Niall kicked madly in between fences and made handbrake turns, getting the pony to jump off one hindleg. They won by two and a half seconds. If this had been a long galloping course the bigger horse would have had the advantage with its longer strides. Anything over fourteen hands was okay for riding clubs.

The Open jumping came next, and these riders jumped against the clock to decide places; a man named Hugh Roe won. Madeline watched and learned.

After the final rosettes had been presented and all horses were put away, the club members gathered to drink tea or orange juice and chat. The young people all owned their horses, which was why Madeline hadn't met them at the riding school.

"We have a serious item for discussion," said Mrs Conroy to the group. "The committee has decided that this year we should put in an application to the National Lottery for funding." She had gained everyone's attention. "The Lottery grants funds to community groups in areas such as heritage, sports, and youth work. Horses are part of Ireland's heritage. Sports and youth work tie in together; giving young people an interest and an incentive to train benefits not just the individual and their family, but society as a whole. Teaching young people to be responsible for animals and to act as a team is hugely important, and will benefit them in later life when they can put Riding Club wins on their CV. While the Club is for anyone over sixteen, I think we'll all agree that there aren't enough activities for young people in the county, especially if they're not playing Gaelic sports."

Everyone was nodding.

"In times of financial recession we don't want to keep asking members to put their hands in their pockets. Horses cost money to keep. We could do a lot with more funding. Better fences. A light beam timer instead of stopwatches. We could hold more shows. Training sessions in areas like stable management, dressage, western pleasure riding and cross country. We could enter more inter-club team contests. All the money would not be spent on prizes..." there were a few laughs and murmurs "...but we could certainly buy some larger trophies as perpetual cups or shields. And no doubt we'd think of other ideas – like tack vouchers and club sweatshirts. Anyway, the application can be prepared by the committee, but it would look a lot better if we had a good full membership and participation, and sent out good teams to represent us and show we have a top standard. This would give us the best chance of being accepted for a grant. Does everyone agree?"

"Yes," the members told her, Madeline included.

"We're holding a pony show here next week, they are great fund-raisers and all hands will be welcomed."

"Aren't we lucky to have the use of Hugh Roe's land?" commented Gary as they headed back to the horsebox.

Madeline hadn't given thought to this matter. She looked around at the grassy, gently sloping field, the hedges and lane leading to the road. Blackbirds flitted among the hawthorns and ash trees in the hedgerow while bumblebees droned gently around the verge wildflowers, landing on buttercups, getting lost inside foxgloves.

"Yes," she said. "Yes we are."

Gary must have heard of the application and he'd been doing his bit to get another young person into the club, she now realised. Well, if it gave her something to do for summer, and it gave her horses, she would do her best to help too. Imagine being able to say that she'd helped her club to win a coveted Lottery grant. Even if it did mean teaming up with farm eejits who talked about silage and thought hurling was the greatest sport in the world.

CHAPTER FOUR

Karen arrived punctually at the livery yard fifteen minutes before Jen was due to depart for the horse show. The blonde girl was oiling the hooves of a black mare, which was plaited and groomed with the professional touch of showing people.

"Ready in a minute," Jen called. "Would you check that Alabama isn't biting her cover?"

Karen went to see and found the chestnut docilely nibbling hay, mane and tail plaited, hooves oiled and light summer sheet in place. She reported.

"The cover just makes their coats glossy, keeps dust off," said Jen, putting the lid on her tin of oil. "All set I think – Shay's gone off to Dore Hill already." The second trailer and jeep were parked in the gateway in preparation. Jen led Alabama to the trailer and showed her the feed bucket. The mare fussed, rolling her eyes with suspicion at the ramp of the trailer. Karen led out the other mare which, being older, loaded easily. Alabama watched and listened to the sound of the mare eating. Jen fastened a strap behind the black rump and enticed the chestnut to step onto the ramp. Karen followed instructions, using the long rein to push the chestnut's quarters up the ramp until she loaded. Quickly Karen secured the back strap before she could change her mind, while Jen fed her.

The girls arrived at their show to find ranks of truck horseboxes and trailers lining three sides of a large field. Two jumping arenas were in use, one for major competitions and one for novices, with two sets of loudspeakers, and in the next field showing was in progress.

"I don't jump, except for Working Hunter," mentioned Jen. "I just don't have time for all the training involved. But Shay told me to bring all your mare's documents in case you decide to have a try."

"Not at that height," gasped Karen, getting a glimpse of a monstrous course.

"That's probably Grade C and D," judged Jen. "The Grand Prix will be later. This is the novice course over here."

Karen watched a few showing classes, which seemed to drag on forever since she didn't know any of the people or horses involved. Whole families were attending, eating picnic lunches on blankets and enjoying the day with their horses. Mobile hamburger stands catered for watchers and competitors alike, and an ice-cream van did a brisk trade. Karen shared coffee and sandwiches with Jen. When her class drew near she helped to unload and tack Alabama. The snaffle bridle with no martingale and a saddle without numnah or cloth were required. A brown leather girth was also appropriate.

"I thought that wide white girth looked well on her," queried Karen.

"It does," agreed Jen. "But for showing classes you and your horse have to look plain and just like everyone else, or you won't be looked at by the judges. No coloured browbands or girths, no cloths or bandages or boots."

Karen, who'd come dressed in jodhpurs and white shirt, now donned stock, long leather riding boots and a black jacket with a new hunting cap.

"Aren't you lucky to have such lovely parents," Jen couldn't help saying. "I hope you get a rosette for them – couldn't they come today?"

"No -" Karen fiddled with the folds of her stock and added a gold stock-pin, watching her actions in the car wing mirror. "They're wonderfully generous, really. But Dad has a business meeting in Bristol and Mum had to arrange something for the parish – something or other."

Alabama was excited and jigged and poked her head up in the air.

"It's all new to her," Jen said. "Would you like me to walk around on her until she settles?"

"No, thanks." Karen fought the urge to surrender the nervous young mare. "I'll take her easy – I won't go far."

"Keep patting her and talking."

Eventually Alabama got tired of being constantly on the boil. She simmered down and allowed her rider to take proper charge, cantering with good manners in a clear space. Jen beckoned; Karen had to hand her number to the ring steward before entering the show ring.

There were more than a dozen young horses, all plaited and gleaming. They walked anticlockwise until everyone was present and the judges gave the signal to trot. After a couple of rounds they all cantered, some now revealing better or worse schooling. Karen had to work constantly to keep Alabama in good shape, trying to look effortless. A horse in front bucked but the chestnut didn't twitch an ear. When they returned to a walk, Karen kept one eye on the judges and steward, and tried to make her mare walk smartly, not slop along or stare at the onlookers. She was called in fifth and made up the front row of six, while the other horses lined up behind them. The steward politely told the back row that the judge wouldn't have time to ride all the horses and if they liked to leave now, that was fine. Taking the hint, the riders thanked her and, touching caps to the judges, filed out of the arena. Karen breathed a sigh of relief. She had to unsaddle and after inspection, resaddle and watch a judge, a short light man who wouldn't strain a young horse's back, mount and ride smartly around the arena. Nobody asked the youngsters to gallop. The chestnut mare wasn't perfect but behaved herself and kept her place. The sixth rider got a lavender rosette; Karen's was pink and fourth was green.

"Well done," Jen praised them. "What a good start."

The black mare was next for action; Jen went to warm up while Karen stayed with Alabama, who was whinnying because she'd been left alone in the box.

"Remember," Jen called, "if you leave, she doesn't know whether any of us will ever come back to her. Horses are herd animals. Keep her company and give her a little grass."

Karen sat watching an Amateur jumping class nearby. The riders who jumped clear were drawn for a jump-off against the clock, going all–out on keen, fast horses to vocal encouragement from the crowd. Amateurs couldn't receive money but were given rosettes, with physical prizes such as a bottle, a voucher for feed and a few grooming tools.

"Could I jump in amateur classes?" Karen enquired of Jen after congratulating her on a third place.

"No, not until you're older," answered the blonde girl. "You'd be surprised, the competition is very tough. But they're announcing a nought to fifteen points class, for beginner horses, so you could walk the course if you like. There's a money prize to divide between double clears."

Karen walked the course, which had been dropped right down to a handy eight-fence track with one double and nothing off-putting like walls or stiles.

"I could jump that even on Merry," she told herself. "And if I'm on horses now I should go ahead in horse classes." She hadn't the nerve to skip the queue with her paperwork but hadn't long to wait to make the entry. Jen mounted her on Alabama, this time with snaffle bit, flash noseband, saddle check and running martingale. In the busy practice arena, with ten other young horses cantering and jumping two fences, bucking or knocking poles or refusing, the chestnut began to fuss with the bit and sweat. Karen had to queue for a low fence, follow on the heels of a horse and hope that the fence would still be intact when she arrived. Checking her girth one more time, Karen revised her course plan and entered the arena. Alabama, who had never seen a jumping arena, threaded her way between the fences, looking at them all and spooking at the timing device. She jumped slowly and awkwardly, cat-jumping twice and hitting two poles.

"That was disastrous," muttered Karen as Jen took the mare's rein.

"Not at all," the blonde girl assured her, "quite good for her first time. New course and field, and out there on her own; at least she didn't refuse. Give her a pat and she'll do a lot better next time."

"I hope so," sighed Karen. She was suddenly exhausted, and her young horse seemed just as tired. They cooled her down and put on a light cover in case she'd get chilled travelling. "She did look beautiful," added Karen. "Thank you for all the grooming and plaiting."

"All part of the job." Jen had been up early, with two horses to plait and groom and all the yard work to do as well.

"Mum, Alabama did really well at showing. She got a fifth place and there were dozens in her class. All the ones ahead of her had shown lots of times before."

44

"Fifth?" wondered Mrs Langourne, eyeing the rosette. The pale pink colour not only faded against strong colours, it clashed with Karen's hair. "Was everything done properly for you? Nothing slipshod?"

"Everything was just perfect. She'll improve with experience, everyone said so."

"Who was the judge? Anyone local?"

"No, Mum, I don't think so."

"Was it a very big show?"

"Oh yes, there were thousands of people there and all kinds of jumping and showing all day."

Mrs Langourne pursed her lips.

"Didn't you jump?"

"Yes, I took her into a Grade E but we just tipped a fence. She'll get better with experience."

"Is E the best grade then?"

Niall bedded down Tigger in his converted calf-shed and fed him extra carrots; he couldn't feed a pony too much oats or nuts. The dun mustn't even be grazed on the lush cattle pastures, for the highly fertilised grasses and clover would flood his system with protein and carbohydrate and give him laminitis, or founder as country folk called inflamed hooves. Greedy as most ponies, Tigger never knew when to stop eating. He was turned out on after-grass when a cut of hay or silage had been lifted, or in stubble fields.

The boy went across the yard whistling, watching barn cats, pied or striped, slink around doors and bales as they hunted mice. A dog barked once, in the nearest house, and one of Niall's dogs barked in reply. Another dog across the valley took up the message; sometimes a chain of barks would travel up and down the darkened valley. The trick was to know which bark was communication and which signalled an alarm.

Pushing open the kitchen door, Niall wiped his feet before stepping into the realm of electric light. Noise assailed his ears at once and he went through the kitchen to the spacious living room. His father looked up from his old armchair and newspaper. The youngest members of the family were glued to some DVD on the television screen; his mother knitted in her chair by the empty fireplace and Granny had gone up to bed. Sean's chair was empty but he had probably gone out with his friends, to a dance or a party.

"Well done, our Niall," his father greeted him with a smile. The family made Niall text home the results. "Tell us when there's a real big occasion and we'll all take the day to watch. Mind, you'd better get a grand trophy that day."

"Inter Club challenge," agreed Niall, placing his red rosette on the mantel, streamers floating in the draught from the chimney.

"Think it's going to hold fine until we get the hay cut, eh? See any meadows cut today?"

Niall answered, then told the family about the proposal to apply for National Lottery grant funding.

"Oh aye," said his father, considering.

"Be good to get some money into the townland," was his mother's opinion, "this recession is draining the place of young people by emigration. Anything to bring in a bit of cheer."

"Do you get the money to spend?" a sibling wanted to know.

"No," said Niall, "but I might win nicer prizes, like a voucher for a tack shop."

"That's what they should do. 'Stead of buying things made in China. Keep it in the community." Mr Johnson approved. "You know, if more money was put in like that, farmers wouldn't have to sell land for housing." This was a sore point.

"Only one farmer nearby has done that," Niall reminded his dad.

"And see what happened. The Langournes came from the city and built a luxury ranch-style bungalow so they could live the good life. They sold the rest of the land to a housing estate developer to fund the bungalow. Then in the middle of the development the banks all crashed. Nobody could get a mortgage to buy a house in the townland where they grew up. The houses were left half-built and the few people who'd moved in were left living on a ghost estate."

"You can't blame the Langournes for the bank collapse," said Mrs Johnson without looking up from her knitting.

Shay checked all the top doors were closed and bolts home; checked the troughs and barrels were full in case of fire. He set barley to steep by measuring a bucket full of the light golden grain and pouring it into a plastic dustbin, adding a bucket of water. He turned off the lights and closed the feed-room, locking the precious tack away behind two stout padlocks, and kicked aside the dishes from which Jen fed the cats. Leaving the yard, he passed through a gate to his small stone cottage. Turning on the lights, he prepared a pot of tea and sat down to catch up on the television news before going to bed. Letters, schedules, magazines and newspapers crowded his tables, and a cardboard box in the corner held rosettes as varied as liquorice allsorts, tossed in as they had been won.

Jen turned the key in her front door and went in, hung up her coat and took her riding clothes upstairs to sort for washing, and came down again to her elderly parents.

"Kettle's on," her mother greeted her. "Have a good day? Oh, third? Yellow is third isn't it? Well done."

Her father came to see.

"I don't think you get a chance," he grumbled. "Every time you bring on a horse to a good level, that man sells it. What about your chances?"

"Oh Dad, I'm not ambitious."

"You should have gone to Dublin years ago, made something of yourself," he muttered.

Too late now, Jen thought but didn't say. Her mother now had Parkinson's and brittle bones. A bad combination. Parkinson's Disease made the sufferer shaky. Her father had survived a cancer scare, which had caused both her parents to drop their smoking habits, and he had scheduled checkups twice a year. Jen had taken over some of the housework.

"I never would have made Aga Khan teams," she said instead. "And there's no money in keeping horses, only in selling them – to the Langournes, to England or anywhere. In Scandinavia and Germany they have vast indoor shows all year 'round. Here the prize money is virtually nil at lower levels, and the bills come in all year. I don't give the horses stable names any more... too easy to get attached."

"How did that Langourne girl get on?" wondered her mother, holding the back of a chair to help steady herself.

"Well enough, fifth showing which pleased her; a bad round jumping which didn't. She expected too much."

"Pots of money," complained her father.

"The girl is nice enough," said Jen with a frown. "Strange, but I almost feel sorry for her."

"Now get matters straight," insisted her father. "You work all hours and all days, even Christmas Day. You don't get paid a fraction of what you're worth."

"Nobody in horses does," said Jen. "We're nuts – all of us. But what other jobs are there anyway? Kettle's boiling – I'll just have a cheese toastie and go to bed."

Sitting up in bed that night, Madeline spread out a couple of books on the quilt and read the jumping section in each. They all offered basic instruction and one had stable management as well; she knew the contents almost by heart. Firm as they were about the correct positions for riding and jumping, none of them offered any help as to actual competitions. Her horizons had suddenly expanded, from earnest circles around an instructor to negotiating a course in public. Mrs Kelly came upstairs and paused on the landing.

"Madeline, are you awake?" The bedside light cast a faint glow onto the landing carpet.

"Yes, Mum. I'm fine."

Mrs Kelly peeped around the door.

"Are you sure you didn't want us to watch you today?"

"No, really, wait until I'm better. Gary says I'll improve quickly now with every competition."

"Okay dear. Do tell us when. 'Night...."

CHAPTER FIVE

Madeline practised hard all week, except for Monday, since Gary said it wasn't a good idea to work a horse straight after a show, and Saturday, so as to keep Moonrock fresh for Sunday. On the Saturday she and Gary drove to Dore Hill's grounds and assisted with the pony show. The teacher explained the jumping rules as they arose.

"The bell's rung to stop her, because when the pony refused he pushed down the poles. They have to be rebuilt and the bell will ring when she can try again.

"That boy is eliminated, not because he fell off, which gives faults, but because the pony ran out of the arena." Gary acted as starter and Madeline as assistant starter and assistant course builder.

"I wish I'd competed when I was a child," observed Madeline. "I'd have got so much fun from it, and learnt so much."

"Why didn't you?" wondered Gary as they waited for a new class to start.

"It was never mentioned at the riding school. Always lessons, but no goal at the end of training. Of course if I'd had my own pony it might have been different."

"Some kids are too competitive – maybe they're from a horsey family. You'll see them scowling if they knock a pole or finish second. Keep it in perspective."

The following day the pony jumping course was used again with slight alterations. Moonrock had rolled in his stable and stained his coat, and not all the persuasion of warm soapy water would remove the stable-mark. He was however becoming steadily fitter and slimmer, and no longer puffed when he was ridden. Gary was increasing the hard feed to keep up his energy and muscles. His rider had also become stronger and fitter, and she had no trouble today with remembering the course.

"Double clear round," echoed across the field.

Madeline lined up with the other double clear Primary riders to receive a red rosette. That was all there was to it? She knew now that she could succeed, and she would never again be overawed by the mere thought of competing.

Shay had his young brown horse ready for Intermediate fences and he brought Karen along to introduce her to the club. The secretary welcomed her.

"I need to know how much experience you have to assign your level. Did you jump high grade classes on ponies?" asked Maeve Conroy.

"No," answered Karen, patting Alabama.

"Take Pony Club exams, or do one-day events?"

"No – I went to a Pony Club camp and got a little trophy for musical chairs."

"Dressage?"

"No – mainly I hacked or showed."

"In that case you can probably start as Intermediate, to give your young horse a good introduction. Is this her first show? She's a real beauty."

Karen smiled, suddenly proud.

"Actually, we went to the SJAI show last week." Realising that this might sound condescending, as though she had nowhere better to go this week, she added hastily, "I wanted to put her in a showing class to start with."

"I expect she did well. Do you intend to jump SJAI classes this year though?"

"Yes," answered the girl. "We went in a nought to fifteen points class last week, it was very small."

"You rode in a Grade E? That makes you Open in Riding Club terms."

"I did - but we didn't go clear."

"That's not the point." Mrs Conroy sounded irritated. "Ride in one Grade E, even nought to fifteen, and you might as well have a BHSAI exam. That's the rule."

"I didn't know," gasped Karen, hoping the secretary wouldn't think she'd been trying to get away with a lower grade.

"Shay should have explained it to you." The woman made notes. "You're paid up as a member here and can enter a class today. What do you want to ride in?"

"I'd better enter in whatever you think I should be in," said Karen humbly.

"Open? You could go in a smaller class hors concours if you wish, but then you're not allowed compete in your own class."

Karen felt bewildered.

"Open's fine."

Alabama attracted all eyes as the girl rode her around the practice arena. Her mane and tail were plaited again and her hooves oiled; her light chestnut coat gleamed and tack shone. Her saddle cloth had Karen's initials printed on it. Upon hearing of the mare's turnout for the showing class, Mrs Langourne had sent a brown envelope to the groom, which had contained a ten euro note. Putting two and two together and making ten euros, Jen had spared no effort this time either, and insisted on taking a photo of Karen and the mare ready to ride, on her phone.

"I'll mail this on to you and you can send it to your friends."

"Wow," murmured Madeline. "Who is that?"

"I don't know her," answered Gary as he affixed Moonrock's frayed nylon halter to let the cob graze, "but Shay said last week that he had a new rider coming."

"She must be a millionaire."

"I think they're well off all right."

Niall had a tough time controlling Tigger, since the pony enjoyed speed so much that he tended to try to cut corners even in the first round. Today the dun was more ebullient than usual and leaned hard on his snaffle, which then became ineffectual. With his thick, strong neck, the pony had more power than even the wiry boy. Niall found himself coming completely wrong towards a double and pulled the reins hard; the jointed bit clamped tight on Tigger's tongue in a nutcracker action which so upset the pony that he threw his head up and forgot the fence. Too late he took off and caught the pole with his knees. Four faults, first round. Niall was disgusted with himself. Tigger would probably have got over the fence somehow if left to his own devices, however impetuous. He cantered straight on to the pocket after finishing, but his action scared a chestnut mare by the rope just inside the pocket, and she shied away violently and tried to bolt. The girl on board, taken by surprise, only just managed to sit tight and regain control.

"Niall!" bellowed the starter, a stout man. "Come back here!" Niall, by now halfway across the practice arena, reined in and returned.

"Listen here, young lad," boomed the starter. "You must never canter out of the ring like that. Stop in front of the pocket and walk out when you're sure the way is clear. You may have a handy pony, but other people here have young horses that scare easily, and you almost caused a serious accident."

The boy, indignant at first at the scolding, gradually saw the sense of the matter. He hadn't even looked, he'd been so annoyed. Might as well cross the road without checking for traffic.

"I'm sorry, I didn't mean it."

"Well go and tell that girl on the chestnut."

The chestnut however recognised the dun as the one that had come charging madly towards her, and was reluctant to let him close, whitening her eyes and flattening her ears.

"Excuse me," said Niall to Karen. "I'm sorry if I upset your mare. I didn't mean to."

Alabama switched her tail furiously, a sign that she intended to kick, and shifted her feet.

"Would you be more careful in future?" was all Karen could manage to say.

Niall turned around and trotted away, deciding that he had no wish to stay around that girl. He'd recognised her and he didn't intend to get friendly with the blow-in Langournes.

Shay completed two steady, careful clear rounds. Karen watched the fences being raised and wished she'd put Alabama in the Intermediate. The mare practised well enough but in the ring stared at everything, jumped 'green' meaning too big, came back to a trot several times and often cantered on the wrong leg. Despite Karen's best efforts they hit both parts of the double.

"Know what you should've done," said Shay, "you should've put her in the Intermediate."

Thanks a million, thought Karen.

"But if you ask the judges they might let you school around in the arena after the class. I'll lower a fence or two and you can just give her a pop." The judges being agreeable, they proceeded and got some quite good jumping from the mare.

A Handy Hunter was in progress in the second arena, which had hosted Working Hunter ponies on the previous day. Novice and open were the only grades here, and Madeline had been practising keenly. Moonrock jumped a couple of low rustic fences neatly, and halted while the rider dismounted, crossed his stirrups and led him through a gateway, opening and closing the gate as she went. He stood still while she remounted, they jumped a double of brush, halted while she dismounted and ran up her stirrups. She led him confidently into a single horse box and they waited in there for ten seconds before backing out, when the girl mounted from a block. There were two more fences to clear, a gate and a narrow stile, then a right-angled corner fence by a hedge which required two bouncing jumps. They finished without fault.

"Excellent," Gary praised. "Best fun Moonrock's had all week. I don't know if anybody could beat that." Nobody did, and Madeline won the novice section. She'd even beaten Niall, as his pony disliked the horsebox. Many horses were chary of loading into a strange box. The town girl had beaten the farm lad, she thought, mentally cheering.

Two red rosettes at once! There were stars in Madeline's eyes as she clutched both rosettes and patted Moonrock.

"He was so good about loading," she told the cob's owner. "But all the time we were in the trailer, he kept nudging me for carrots."

"Better give him one now. He knows he deserves it."

"Can I put the rosettes on his bridle?" She felt terribly proud.

"Good lord, no," returned Gary. "That might be all right for children's ponies, or showing champions, but it's not done for jumpers or riding clubs. Too much like showing off, although I know you wouldn't mean that."

"I see." Madeline felt deflated. "What can I do then?"

"Acceptable conduct," decided Gary, "includes putting the rosettes in your jacket pocket or jeans pocket with just the ribbons trailing out."

Madeline promptly pocketed the rosettes – one in each pocket, so people could see that she'd won two.

Eamonn was impressed, though he pretended not to be, when his sister produced the red rosettes that evening. She didn't flaunt them, just left them on the mantelpiece with the ribbons trailing carelessly over the edge, which he found far more impressive than if she'd been showing them around to everyone. Madeline told him the number of people competing in each class, and he couldn't think of any smart remarks. Evidently his sister really was good at riding.

CHAPTER SIX

"Mum, the club's holding an evening barbecue, for members only," Madeline mentioned. "They were all so friendly and congratulated me, and several people said they hoped to see me at the barbecue. Is it okay for me to go?"

Mrs Kelly, rolling pastry for apple pies, hesitated. The girl was peeling apples and greasing dishes, as the oven hummed warmly. Madeline had a streak of flour across one cheek and sprinkling of white across her black t-shirt.

"Better ask your father, dear."

Madeline asked her father.

"Better ask your mother."

"I did. She said to ask you."

"Well, I don't know. I don't know all these people or what they're likely to get up to or what they drink."

"They're very ordinary people, Dad, mostly. Gary's going. Do you want to talk to him?"

"I'll leave that to your mother. And if she says you've been up to any nonsense, you can't go."

Madeline's mother chatted to Gary on his phone and had her worries allayed. He promised to return the girl by eleven o'clock at the latest, and suggested that she bring along whatever soft drinks she enjoyed.

"It'll probably rain," prophesied Eamonn.

The evening of the barbecue was cloudy but dry, and a spectacular sunset of reds, oranges and pinks glowed across half the sky as Gary and

Madeline fed Moonrock and settled him down for the night. The cob chewed contentedly in his bin as they left. Waving goodbye to Gary's parents, the pair drove down to the road, into the setting sun.

"Rachel will be here next weekend," said Gary. "You'll like her."

"Does she ride?"

The girl had heard a lot about Gary's fiancée, who was an airline cabin crew member and spent a lot of time abroad.

"She used to. But she hasn't a horse and she wouldn't be able to fit much into her schedules anyway."

"Where are you going to live when you get married?"

"The school where I teach isn't far from the airport and up to this I've been renting a flat during term-time. But we're getting a house between us, renting to start and then buying. Just a small place."

Reaching Dore Hill's field, they parked the car and strolled towards a little knot of people around a fire and barbecue. Everyone wore jeans and sweatshirts. Rooks circled, cawing raucously, as they found perches for the night in tall ash or lime trees at the end of the field. Greetings were called, plastic cups of various drinks dispensed and paper plates of food were being readied. Baked potatoes in tinfoil were cooking in the fire while sausages, burgers and kebab skewers from cool-boxes were being placed on the barbecue. Salad leaves, sliced tomatoes, bread rolls and sauces sat in dishes on a folding table. A guitar and bodhran provided music.

"What kind of music do you like Madeline?" asked Niall, thinking that he'd better make an effort. She wasn't a bad looking girl, he supposed, quite nice really. Not to compare with the pop star girls in glittery sports tops that you saw on the internet and TV, but she was slim and sporty looking. And the stars were plastered with make-up and hair gel anyway.

"Rock music," said the girl. "InXS, Guns N'Roses, great tracks though they're older now, Robbie Williams, Lady Gaga and Coldplay. You?" She was hoping Niall might have some decent music in his phone or iPod, because she'd forgotten her favourite tracks. When she saw him up close, he was halfway decent looking, she considered, not tall but strong-shouldered and his arms were muscled when you saw him in a t-shirt. There was a slight shadow along his jawline, as if he shaved a couple of days a week.

"Country and Irish. Not, like, Christy Moore, he's too old but the recent lads."

Oh well, they each thought.

"Do you notice who is conspicuous by her absence?" added Niall.

"Who – oh, that red-haired girl?"

"Karen Langourne. Couldn't expect Lady Muck to mix with the likes of us. I'd say smoked salmon is more her style. Have you met Jen? She works at Shay's yard. She's really nice, I'll introduce you."

Madeline wanted to stand up for Karen at first, just on the feminist principle. But she knew nothing about Karen, so maybe the redhead was a Lady Muck. By saying nothing, at least she would seem to be on Niall's side. They didn't have much else in common.

"Someone was asking me how old Moonrock is," she said to Gary later. He'd been leaving her to mix with the younger crowd. "I got the feeling they thought he should be retired."

"He thrives on a bit of light work," said Gary. "Turn the old boy out in a field, day in day out? He'd die of boredom. And he'd stiffen up. A nice light rider over small courses; perfect for the old boy. Better for him to meet other horses too, horses are herd animals. Who was asking?"

"Jen."

"Ah, she's probably hoping Shay could sell me whatever horse she's bringing on, that's all. Don't let it worry you. And I can't afford to keep two horses, what with farrier and feed."

Madeline found that age didn't matter much among horsey people, and she heard a wide range of extraordinary equestrian experiences. Gary dropped her home at five to eleven, and waited until she'd let herself in the door. Maybe it hadn't been a wild party, but she'd enjoyed her evening.

CHAPTER SEVEN

Karen sauntered into the livery yard, wearing corduroy jodhpurs and a neatly tailored shirt in cream and sand, colours which set off her hair to advantage. Alabama's blaze showed just inside the dim stable. Another door was open, and here Karen found Jen grooming the black mare which had won third in showing. As Karen began to say hello, an engine became audible and a smart four-wheel drive towing a double trailer pulled into the yard.

"Oh, they've arrived," said Jen. "I've just got her ready." The mare wasn't plaited. Karen frowned.

"Is she going to a show?"

"She's sold," Jen answered. "These people saw her at that show and came to try her yesterday; Shay made a deal. I'd better offer them a cup of tea; would you mind fetching Shay? He's schooling."

Karen jogged out to the field and waved; Shay, busy putting his young brown gelding through figures of eight, nodded and turned in her direction.

"Someone's come for the black mare," the girl told him.

"Oh, I'll come right in. Don't suppose you'd mind leading this fella around to cool down?"

"Er − okay." Karen's hand trembled as she took the reins. Shay dismounted, settled his cloth cap and slackened the girth.

"Just a few minutes, is all. His stable door's open but I'll send Jen out."

The young horse – Cootehill Lad – was enormous. Tall and powerful, he could have made two of Alabama. Karen ran up the stirrups and led him around on the concrete, metal shoes ringing with every step. All was well until he caught sight of the strange vehicle. He stood stock-still to stare, and not all her nervous tugs on the rein and requests to walk on had any effect. His eyes were fixed on the vehicle and his nostrils flared as he tried to decide whether the unfamiliar object was a threat. Karen patted his neck, but with one jerk of his large head he twitched the reins out of her hand. Snorting his wariness, the gelding backed away from the vehicle. The girl reached for the reins but he threw up his head and continued his evasive actions.

"Karen!" called Jen. "Leave him. Close the gate." Glad to have help, the girl obeyed. By the time she had closed the gate Jen was approaching the big gelding, talking to him in a no-nonsense way, her hands spread out low down. She steadily reached out and took the rein, turning the horse's head away from the vehicle and ordering him to walk. He turned and reluctantly followed her across to his own stable.

"Oh boy," muttered Jen to Karen as she untacked. "I don't know whether he's a real brute or just plain stupid. But he's too big to mess around with; Shay says he'll make an eventer, but I'd be glad to see the back of him if he only went for hunting. Awkward, isn't he?"

Karen agreed. She took the saddle from the blonde girl and moved towards the door; Jen unfastened the throatlatch of the bridle and noseband, then waited for the big horse to lower his head. He stuck his head up in the air, almost touching the roof of the stable.

"I can't take it off, you idiot; put your head down." The horse's eyes held a dreamy expression, as though he had forgotten the bridle. Jen worked the reins up his neck to his poll, and rubbed his crest with one hand while the other held his nose lightly. Eventually the gelding deigned to lower his head and she was able to slip the reins and headpiece over his ears. As the bit left his mouth he jerked his head abruptly and hit off the roof, then jumped with fright.

"Out," panted Jen as she scrambled for the door. The two girls got out and closed the door until the big gelding stopped his erratic movements.

"You big thicko," scolded Jen. "Now you see, Karen, why I don't leave a water bucket in his stable."

Shay pocketed his cheque, handed back ten euros luck money with a smile, and ushered his clients out to the yard, where they fitted their own headcollar to the black mare and loaded her into the trailer, enticing her with sugar-lumps. Jen helped to lift the ramp and gave the mare a parting pat; the new owners left, wearing delighted expressions.

"Shay," asked Jen, "don't leave that big horse with anyone else in future. He's too awkward."

"Awkward?" Shay blinked. "He just needs proper handling. He didn't hurt himself?"

"Not this time," returned Jen darkly. "Karen, I think we could do with a cup of tea ourselves."

The redhead followed meekly into the cottage and accepted a cup of strong tea in a chipped mug.

"Aren't you lucky," said Jen morosely as she sipped. "The better you do with Alabama, the less chance there is that she'll be sold from under you."

Karen didn't know what to say, so she said nothing.

"She was only a gardener's daughter, but she wouldn't walk out with a rake," commented Gary, appearing around the corner of the stable, and Madeline, who was raking up loose straw, had to giggle. "You know what a rake means?" he added.

"Of course. I read some historical romances. This is Eamonn," she introduced her brother, and Gary solemnly shook hands. "He wanted to see Moonrock."

"How fast can he go?" queried the boy, standing at a safe distance from the kindly grey head.

"He's not a car," chided Gary. "We're going to school him now – would you like a ride?"

"No, not really," said the boy, shrugging. But when he saw Madeline ride as though this was the greatest fun in the world, cantering in circles without stirrups and dropping her reins as she popped down a little grid, then jumping properly over poles balanced on oil drums, he changed his mind.

Moonrock turned out to be wider, taller and hairier than Eamonn had expected, and he felt glad of the riding cap when he glanced down at the moving ground. Madeline led the cob at a steady walk, and after a few minutes they trotted to let Eamonn feel the bumpiness of the pace. The boy decided as he dismounted, that riding wasn't so easy as it appeared, but at least now he could boast to his pals that he had ridden.

"Madeline, knock, knock," he asked.

"Who's there?" The girl's tone was resigned.

"Kylie."

"Kylie who?"

"That's show business."

The other two laughed.

"She listens to really daft music," Eamonn told Gary. "Heavy metal."

"Looks like it," said Gary, because in today's heat Madeline was wearing a black t-shirt bearing the words Appetite For Destruction. "That sounds slightly familiar, in a non-musical format."

"Non-musical is right," giggled Eamonn.

Gary took out his phone and made a swift internet search for the phrase.

"Found it. A quotation from John Steinbeck, in *The Winter Of Our Discontent.* Which title is itself a quotation from Shakespeare."

"You're a teacher all right," muttered Eamonn.

"I mostly read books on horses," Madeline told them.

The stable management instruction books were coming in useful, as Madeline had been comparing Moonrock's turnout with other horses and decided that his image needed smartening. In the pictures, horse didn't have long, thick, uneven manes which fell to either side of their crest, nor big bushy tails, hirsute ears and whiskery muzzles.

"Instead of schooling," she requested on the next wet day, "could I tidy up his mane and tail a little?"

Gary found her a metal mane comb in the grooming box in his small tackroom.

First Madeline combed Moonrock's mane free of tangles, then decided which side of the crest most of it lay. The books said that plaits ought to lie to the right for showing, but that didn't concern her. The books also told her that long or underneath hair was older and should be pulled first. The comb helped to separate the old hair, and she pulled out a few strands at a time to judge the cob's reaction. He ignored this, so emboldened, she wound a slightly larger tuft around the comb, giving it a sharp tug. The old, dull, dry hairs loosened easily and she soon found what size tuft she could take.

Gary went back to the house to make them tea, and when he returned, Madeline was standing on a milk-crate beside Moonrock, working steadily.

"My arms were getting tired of reaching up," she explained.

"Great idea. Don't do too much in one day, or he'll get sore."

Over a few days the cob's mane was shortened and thinned. His tail received the same attention; the girl used the comb to sort the hairs at the top of the tail, and pulled a couple between her fingers from the sides. Gary was emphatic that a scissors must not be used, claiming that the cob would grow spiky hairs like a punk rocker. Madeline had to believe him because the book cautioned against scissors, but she ended up with sore and blistered fingers. The scissors were only used to trim the end of the tail where it got straggly.

Moonrock's grey ears had long hairs sticking out from their interiors. Here scissors were permissible, and with Gary's guidance the girl pressed the sides of the ears together and trimmed off any hairs which protruded. She thinned the cob's forelock and cut the bottom of his tail square, just below the level of his hocks. His white whiskers made his head look untidy, but Gary asked her to trim them leaving a couple of centimetres on the whiskers around the cob's eyes and muzzle.

"He'd bump into things if he didn't have whiskers. And they help him to graze or eat his feed. He's not able to see anything under his nose, you realise."

"He can't?"

"Can you? And look what a long, wide head he has, with his eyes right up on the sides of his head to watch for predators. He can't see directly in front or behind either. That's why you should always approach a horse from one side, and talk as you move around him. Let him see you and keep letting him know where you are, and you're most unlikely to get kicked."

Moonrock now looked a different horse – younger and neater.

"Well done," commented Gary approvingly. "I would never get around to doing all that – you've made a big difference."

"Every time I did some pulling, I gave him a carrot as a reward for standing still when I'd finished."

"Know what he needs next? Shoeing. Those shoes have grown down, see, and that one is loose. He doesn't do much road work so I get least two removes out of each set; a remove is every six to eight weeks."

The blacksmith drove up in his van few days later, and Madeline held Moonrock while the farrier removed the shoes, trimmed the feet and filed them with a big flat rasp, made sure the shoes were strong and level and deftly nailed them back in place. He turned down the ends of the nails – clenches – and twisted off the points with a hammer dainty enough for a leprechaun cobbler, then rasped the nails until they fitted flush with the hoof wall.

"This old boy's looking well," he complimented, "must be the new groom, eh?" Gary laughed and admitted that this was the truth. "Lovely horse to shoe," the farrier added, slapping Moonrock's shoulder approvingly. "Fair holds up the legs himself."

"Are some of them difficult?" wondered Madeline.

"Oh aye. Shod one big devil recently for Shay Broughton and nearly strained my back. He'd lift his foot all right, but then he'd lean down on me to let me take his weight – must be half a tonne of horse pressing on my back and shoulder. Not funny. And when I'd the nails just set into the shoe he'd pull the foot out of my hand – ripped my hand with a point, see that scratch, and made it hard to shoe him without laming him. A nail only has to go slightly wrong and that's a lame horse for a month."

"Can girls be farriers?" enquired Madeline.

"I know of a few," returned the man seriously. "Mostly men do it because of the heavy work involved, but anyone can do a special training course and apprenticeship. Interested?"

"I'll have to finish school first," she said, pleased that the big man hadn't made fun of her.

"Horses are a great life," declared the man. "Don't ride 'em myself but I love 'em."

Niall drove the tractor slowly and steadily, hauling a large flat trailer on big wheels. The combine had tossed out bales and left them on the ground for drying; today he picked up the bales from the pyramidal stacks of three which had allowed them to air. Hay was heavy – twice as heavy as straw, especially when green. His older brothers Sean and Jamie pitchforked the bales up onto the trailer and Niall halted at intervals to climb onto the trailer and help stack them. A younger brother appeared, having finished other chores, and the work progressed, the stack growing higher. The sun which had done such an excellent job of drying the cut grass made loading the hay hot work; perspiration ran from Niall's forehead into his eyes. The stringy hay and taut bale twines chafed his hands, and grass stains covered the t-shirt and jeans he wore.

This green hay would have to be stored very carefully, or spontaneous combustion in a heating stack could burn bales and barn. Nor could it be used for several months as it was too green for the horses. Niall's younger brother was keen to demonstrate his strength, but his staying power was limited and he was glad when the older lads decided that they had a full load. The trailer held about 100 bales and the farm might save 5000 in a year. Hay was expensive and scarce now that so many cattle farmers made silage instead, and racehorses in particular needed the finest quality, non-mouldy hay.

"Here, I'll help you down," Niall offered, holding up his arms to his young brother.

"I want to ride back on the load."

"No," said Niall and Sean in the same breath. "That's dangerous," added Niall. "Come on, you can ride in the tractor with me."

"Oh all right… I bet it'll take Tigger all winter to eat this hay."

"It's not all for him," laughed Niall.

CHAPTER EIGHT

Dore Hill ran another show on the next Saturday, and had a hunter show planned for the Sunday. They ran few events during winter or crop-growing time, Gary explained, so they liked to make the most of the summer. Madeline was pleased to receive one or two compliments on Moonrock's turnout, even though she hadn't plucked up the nerve to plait.

Once more Madeline achieved a double clear round, so she won the red rosette for Primary. She noticed that Niall got a double clear also but was beaten by half a second in the jump-off. Mrs Conroy beamed as she presented the red rosette to her own son, Turlough. Shay took his young horse into Open and had eight faults in the second round. Karen had four faults in the first round.

"That mare should do well in the hunter show tomorrow," Gary addressed Alabama's rider. The girl smiled and kept moving. Gary looked after her as she returned to Shay's trailer, then shook his head.

Karen unsaddled Alabama – pretty, plaited Alabama – and let her pick at grass, turning her black-jacketed back to everyone so they couldn't see the tears of disappointment and frustration on her cheeks.

Madeline and Gary had no sooner drawn up in front of the stable than a young woman appeared from the house. She caught Gary's hand as he got out of the car and he hugged her warmly before turning to introduce Madeline.

"Rachel, Madeline – Madeline, Rachel."

"Glad to know you," said the air stewardess, smiling, "I hope you're keeping him out of trouble." She had shoulder-length jet black hair, carefully styled and held with gold clips; her light blue summer dress with dark abstract patterns showed tanned arms and legs. Her eyes and lips bore makeup and a necklace of blue and green coral completed her outfit. Madeline liked her at once, though she felt unavoidably shy. Her own shirt and jeans suddenly seemed inadequate.

"What a wonderful job you have," was all she could reply.

"Cabin crew means being a glorified waitress," chuckled Rachel. "Sure, I travel – but mostly what I see are airports. There's so much routine and schedules, and hassle if anything goes wrong. The turnaround times are tight so there's no time to relax. The perks are the best part – cheap standby flights for holidays."

Rachel stroked Moonrock as he was put into his stable, remarking that he was as handsome as ever.

"Er -" said Madeline. "If the two of you want to go on, I'll look after Moonrock and put him away for the night."

"There's no hurry," Rachel demurred, but Gary thanked the girl and said that he was glad she was so responsible. They did have plans to make regarding their upcoming honeymoon. He invited her to come in for a cup of tea if she wanted one.

Madeline let Moonrock roll and get a drink; she cleaned out the trailer, shook down more bedding in his stable and added a pile of hay to keep him chewing, then mixed his feed; a scoop each of oats, nuts and molassed sweet feed. Hearing the rattle of nuts in the bucket, Moonrock came to poke his grey nose around the door. She brushed him lightly to remove sweat, then took the tack out of the car and hung it up properly. The numnah was damp with sweat so she set it aside for washing.

"Good night Moonrock," she said, closing the top door, and the cob took his muzzle out of the bin to glance at her, still chewing. Madeline cycled home in the gathering dark, thinking that it would have been nice to have someone her own age around to chat to while she worked.

Karen heated her meal in the microwave and while it hummed, went to talk to her parents. Her father, relaxing in an armchair with the newspaper open to the financial page, glanced up and smiled.

"Have a good day, love?"

"Fair," she replied. "Wasn't the weather glorious?"

Mrs Langourne, tearing her eyes away from a documentary on starving children in refugee camps, agreed.

"I hope you've been protecting your skin – you know you burn so easily." She pressed the remote button to dull the sound. "And did you get a prize today?"

"Ah, well no. We just had four faults, that's only one pole down and they were quite high so…"

"Dear, dear." Her mother frowned. "Karen, we were assured that the mare would be a top-class jumper. I hope we weren't misled?"

"No, no."

"Don't pressure her," interjected Mr Langourne, folding the paper. "These things take time, isn't that so? It's a partnership, and any sport takes practise." His gaze caressed the golfing trophies adorning discreetly recessed shelves and niches; a crystal decanter and glasses, a silver tray, a china figurine – nothing of the type where a golfer swinging perched atop white marble. He had won those also but they weren't suited to the lounge.

"But if the mare isn't good enough," persisted Mrs Langourne.

"She's great," asserted Karen hurriedly. "Several people have been saying how good she'll be. Actually I'm certain it was my fault today, we did come a little fast and that's my job. Oh, there's the microwave bell."

On the following day Karen went with Shay and Jen to the hunter show. This was open to anyone and had been widely advertised, so attendance was high as hopeful contenders for the Dublin Horse Show got in some practise. Alabama had to wear a double bridle and was still green in it despite a week's schooling, over-bending every time the curb was used though the curb chain was slack. By now she had muscled up behind the saddle but she'd been working so much that her fit-looking frame didn't carry the excess fat which was inexplicably popular with judges of hunters. For whichever reason, or all three, Alabama was unplaced, and it was small consolation to Karen that Jen was also excluded from the line-up. Jen rode a green iron-grey gelding, a half-Irish Draught which carried himself well but needed more schooling. Already a big horse, at 16.3 as a five-year-old, Jen had predicted that he would finish well over 17hh.

"He's too Draughty," she complained. "He'll get heavy and won't be able to jump high. If he's to jump, he should have started a year ago."

"Never mind the jumping," Shay told her. "Keep on with working hunter and we'll try to sell him from the American Green Hunter class in the RDS. It's supposed to be only for horses seven-eights Thoroughbred or better, but nearly every year they give the prize to a Draught producer instead." The grey, named Dirk, was a handsome horse with a wonderfully kind nature.

"I don't know why he wasn't placed in light heavyweight," Shay muttered to Jen and Karen. Just then the red-haired girl saw the prize-winners cantering their lap of honour.

"What an ugly horse," she commented – quietly. "How did it ever get first?" The other two followed her gaze. The first-placed hunter in Jen's class was a brown, with probably the largest and bumpiest Roman nose they had ever seen. While they were still gaping, the blue-ribbon horse followed, sporting an almost identical Roman nose.

"I don't believe it," gasped Jen.

"There's your answer," grumbled Shay. "That judge obviously likes Roman-nosed horses – probably breeds them himself – and doesn't even look at anything else." Shay rode his young horse in the heavyweight class, which had attracted only four entries – one of the reasons he regularly rode heavyweights – and won, a just reward for his hours of schooling. Cootehill Lad appeared extremely handsome with the small red rosette fastened to his bridle, and had gained a money prize, besides qualifying for the hunter championship, to be held last.

Jen and Karen both rode in working hunter, wearing snaffles, which helped Alabama. The chestnut gained fifth in a crowded class. Jen, in the next weight, was unplaced as her horse jumped clear but greenly. Shay took second in the heavyweight division. Then Shay won the reserve champion rosette to finish the day – with different judges, the Roman–nosed horses were unplaced. A middleweight gelding was Champion.

Jen explained to Karen that it would be very unusual for a lightweight like Alabama to be Champion.

"The bigger horses 'fill the eye' better, look more impressive," she said. "By the way, all the top prizes have gone to professional producers, as usual."

"I used to think," considered Karen, "that the most beautiful horse just had to go out there and win."

"Fat chance," retorted Jen. "This is a small country. In the Dublin Horse Show a few years ago, I was watching the medium weight hunter gelding, six years or over, class. A certain lady, well known and the wife of an extremely well known producer and dealer, was riding a fairly plain bay. She was relegated to the middle of the back row. Just before the judges sent the back row out of the ring, they realised their mistake, and hastily approached the lady and invited her to join the front row."

"I don't believe it," gasped Karen.

"I wouldn't have either except that I was there. It's all about who you know at the top level. I don't know how ordinary people ever bother to keep showing."

A horrible thought struck Karen. She clutched the working hunter rosette she'd won.

"Jen – nobody could say I got this because of my parents, could they?"

The blonde girl looked blank for a second, then laughed.

"I doubt it – sorry to say this, but whatever influence they might have elsewhere, they don't have any in the horse world."

"Thank goodness," breathed Karen. At least in showjumping, nobody's opinion had to count – just one's own skill and luck.

Madeline went to the hunter show as a spectator, since Gary had assured her that Moonrock could not hope to win showing prizes. She allowed plenty of time for cycling, and arrived early, so she offered to help Mrs Conroy. The secretary was delighted, and Madeline spent the morning in the entry caravan taking money and handing out numbers. In the afternoon she was course assistant for the working hunters. She was surprised when lunch was provided for her, with a choice between chips and hamburger from the hot-food wagon or a selection of filled crusty rolls. Competitors got used to living from a flask and lunchbox.

"This show is a major fund-raiser every year," Mrs Conroy told her. "We support local charities. The judges and stewards have their expenses covered and the rest of us hard workers have lunch. Enjoy it now!"

When Madeline discovered that one of the charities mentioned was the local branch of Riding For The Disabled, she was thrilled.

CHAPTER NINE

The livery yard was crowded with youngsters and their ponies, all ready to hack out together around the fields and lanes. Jen sorted out problems such as girths that wouldn't fit, and checked their hard hats, then saw them out the gate with a reminder to ride single file and only walk while they were on the road. Karen, who'd just arrived, watched thoughtfully.

"Hi. Noisy lot, aren't they?" Jen greeted her. "Your lady's a bit stiff today, she might've overdone it yesterday."

"You don't talk to me the way you talk to the others," commented Karen, "yet some of them are my age."

"Well – I suppose you're more responsible," Jen considered, "more mature. You see, you've got a young horse. You can't carry on any old way like they can. There's a world of difference."

Karen tried to remember herself waving, chatting and shrieking with laughter as the pony riders were doing, twisting in the saddle to chat, slopping along in any position with their ponies' heads in the air. Had she looked and behaved like that? She honestly couldn't remember. Merry seemed a lifetime ago, and feet smaller.

"I've decided to work harder at improving our jumping," she told Jen as they assessed Alabama's soundness. "We're still not getting it together as a partnership. But I don't know what to do. You seem to get on well with new horses so quickly."

"I spend a lot of time with them." Jen eyed the younger girl speculatively. "I don't just mean, riding time. Not meaning to criticise you in the slightest, Karen, because I'm doing a job here. I clean out, I water, feed and groom. I exercise, pick out feet, pull manes and tails and plait. In winter I clip as well. The horses get to know me very well; look forward to seeing me with feed or brushes. I learn all about their nerves and likes and dislikes." She paused. "For instance, Alabama positively loves to have her face brushed. Did you know that?" Without waiting for an answer she turned and walked to the hayshed, where the cats slept and the dapper swallows twittered as they dived in to reach mud nests high on the back wall. Karen remained still, looking at Alabama, who loved to have her face brushed.

The Dore Hill team selectors sat around the table in the Conroys' living room. They needed two teams for the Region's Team Challenge competition. Mrs Conroy held a sheet of paper with Team A and Team B written on top, and Open and Novice down the side. Both teams required two of each grade of competitor.

"We'll put Fiona and Turlough on Team A," decided the club's chairman. "They've been riding very well and consistently and they've plenty of experience." The secretary smiled fractionally as she wrote Fiona Conroy and Turlough Conroy in the appropriate spots. "For the other Open, how about Shay? He won't have to go against the clock on his young horse, Fiona can do that."

"I would agree," spoke up Hannah Brooks, "except that we don't have another good reliable Open rider."

"How about Hugh?" queried the vice-chairman.

"He can't jump on teams," Hannah reminded him, "not with that Grade A horse, retired or not."

"Well, there's always Maire," spoke up Mrs Conroy, but this was met with no great enthusiasm. Maire rode a lazy horse which grew fat as a barrel each summer, and was just as likely to refuse as to jump. His owner, who had two small children, wouldn't have felt safe on anything more lively. She was really enthusiastic and the odd good day did a lot to encourage her. "The team could always discard her score if it was the worst or if she was eliminated."

"She should get some of the condition off that horse," sniffed Hannah.

"Anyway," proceeded the chairman, "Shay could be anchor rider for team B. He wouldn't like to go against the clock on his young horse, but the best novices will be on Team A and his lot can just get experience." This meeting general approval, the names were written.

"Team A needs another novice," pointed out Mrs Conroy. "Niall? He's doing well in the points league."

"I don't agree," said the vice-chairman. "That pony only likes going fast, and tends to resist his rider in the first round. I saw them come unstuck recently. The A team has to be sure of going clear."

"Niall has a lot of experience though...."

"So does Betty."

"Betty's going away as an exchange student to Spain."

"Sinead?" Sinead was agreed upon and Team A was full.

"How about Kevin?" asked Hannah suddenly. "He's got a good few points in the Open league."

"No use," said Mrs Conroy. "He's sent his mare to stud."

"To stud?"

"Well, she's fourteen and he said for a first foal it had better be now or never. She's gone off to a stallion and won't be back for a few weeks, and he's resting her then."

"Forget him then," muttered the chairman. "Who else for B?"

"Bottom of the barrel," scraped up Mrs Conroy, "is our newest recruit, Karen."

"I don't think she's exactly team material," dismissed the vice-chairman. "Wait until she has more experience."

"Novices; Niall. If he jumps two careful clear rounds, we'll consider him for the A team next time," decided the chairman. "Robert said he didn't want to be considered for teams. He hasn't been riding very long."

"There's one or two folks whom we only see a couple of times a year," noted Hannah. "Like when we're running a trophy class, or RDS qualifiers. I'd rather ask regular supporters. After all, the club pays for team entries. Pity we can't call on Caroline Mitchell."

"We have her horse though," said Mrs Conroy suddenly. Everyone stared at her. "Oh, I know his new rider is only Primary, but really I think she'd be able for Intermediate. If she upgraded she could jump on a team."

"That's a bit quick," objected the chairman. "We're not forcing anyone to upgrade."

"But Madeline has been riding for years. She was chatting to me at the hunter show. She's very competent, now she's got the hang of it. And so keen to learn, and willing to help. She won red the last couple of times, and it's not as though Intermediate is a big step."

"Could we depend on her though?" asked Hannah darkly.

"She'd only be on the B team, and they could always discard her score. The horse jumped Open with Gary and he's very reliable."

"We'll say nothing," decided the chairman. "How much time do we have? If she continues to do well, I'll mention it to Gary. I don't want to put pressure on Madeline. Don't forget, the Team Challenge is the most hotly contested event of the year, and she never jumped on a team at all. I don't want her thinking that the Lottery grant rests on her, or anything."

CHAPTER TEN

The latest edition of the club newsletter received careful perusal. This was e-mailed where possible to save postage. Three days were scheduled for: 'RDS qualifiers. Dressage from 11am. Equitation jumping from 1pm.'

"You should go in for those," Jen prompted Karen. "I do every year, and as well as being an incentive to improve one's riding, there's a chance to represent the club in the RDS."

"What's it all about?"

"Each autumn the Royal Dublin Society allows the AIRC to use its grounds for one day, for the sum of one shilling or equivalent in modern money. The clubs all send teams for dressage and for equitation jumping, which is like working hunter but the rider is judged on style."

"What grade am I in dressage?"

"Advanced Intermediate, I imagine. You ought to be lower, but you can't drop by more than one grade. I'm the same, and Open in jumping because I've done some Grade E. I'm too busy now with show horses and livery to bother. When the professionals have five or six Grade E mounts to your one, you don't gain much. But I do equitation jumping all right. We could work together if you like."

"Sure," agreed Karen, nodding, grateful for the older girl's experience. They marked out a dressage arena 20 x 40 metres with poles and placed buckets at each letter. Jen did not need the letters written up, and she insisted on Karen's learning them in order.

"Enter at A always, that's the bottom of the arena. The judges sit at the top, usually in a car, so think of C as the car. Dead centre is X of course. Learn the letters clockwise from A – All King Edward's Horses Can Make Bad Falls. It also helps to remember the sequences MCHEK and BFAKE because you often get asked to trot or canter those."

The two of them practised trotting around the arena and keeping well into the corners, making circles of the correct size and straight lines across the diagonal. Alabama was poor at square halts but her circles were good and as her carriage improved she was easier to ride at sitting trot. With so much showing schooling, she had learned to track up from her hind quarters and carry her head well; her neck muscles were now comfortable in an arching curve. However Karen had to learn to make her aids clearly visible to the judges instead of as discreet as possible.

"Outside leg well behind the girth – heel down, toe forward," Jen would remind her on a corner. "If she resists your hand at any time, for goodness' sake don't let on. Do make her bend her head and neck around on the circle... here's a tip, get ready to send on two strides before the marker. Her legs are so long, she needs a bit of time to sort herself out when you ask for a canter. Give her plenty of notice but don't ease your hand until just before the marker. In that way too, prepare to slow a few strides early."

Shay indulged in dressage, not because he enjoyed it, but because a few prizes added to a horse's value. He worked on Cootehill Lad intermittently, wearing a cloth cap to prevent the top of his head from becoming sunburnt. His gelding worked well one day and badly another, seeming to act stupidly stubborn when he took the notion.

The three of them took turns to ride equitation jumping – trying for a flowing round, with balanced riding on the correct legs, the rider setting up the strides to each fence. Dirk was too green to understand this, preferring to charge ahead and use his strength to take off far away from the fence rather than adjust his stride. Because of this the grey didn't always make a good shape in the air, jumping flat like a hurdler, whereas the other two made basculing shapes over the fences. They landed with their hocks under them, but he landed on his forehand and remained unbalanced for a few strides, and would have been unable to clear higher fences or combinations.

"He'll improve with time and work," Shay analysed. Jen couldn't hope to win a prize, but decided to enter anyway for experience. The fences would not be high.

"Dressage?" asked Gary. "Never did any. There's not much to it, you have to plait and look pretty and trot and canter where you're told. Want to try? I don't think Primary riders can go in for the equitation so you may as well do the other."

"Can't I jump well enough?" wondered Madeline.

"It's not that," consoled Gary, "they just think Primaries have enough to do getting around the course in the right order and leaving the fences standing, without worrying as to balancing and pointing toes at the same time. Most Primaries aren't as confident in the saddle as you – those years in the riding school weren't wasted, you know."

"What's Test 4? It says here, Primary Test 4, Intermediate Test 7, Open Test 12."

"I'll download it from the club site, print off a couple of copies. In the meantime we can get you used to riding around a rectangle."

Guessing at the dimensions, they set out an arena, and Madeline hunted through her books until she found the correct letters and their positions. The two of them tried to decipher the paper test sheet by walking the instructions, having to establish where right became left and what on earth was meant by some of the hieroglyphics. Eventually the girl rode through it with Gary calling instructions. There was nothing complex.

"Moonrock doesn't seem interested," she reported.

"Caroline did some dressage with him."

"How did they do?"

"I don't recall."

Gary talked to his sister in France by Skype that evening and reported to Madeline on the following day.

"Caroline says that Moonrock gets bored with dressage. He'll do it but you mustn't school him too much or he'll start refusing to canter and so on. Learn it by heart and ride big circles, she says. Also – good news! You've permission to borrow her black jacket and white tie, if you fit them."

"Wonderful!" exclaimed the girl. "It's so smart. Are you sure she doesn't mind my riding Moonrock?"

"No, she didn't sound as though she cared. She gets these phases of being interested in things."

In order to fool the cob, the girl practised in among jumps and occasionally popped over a small fence to stop his attention wandering. Madeline had been horrified to discover that she was expected to ride most of the test in sitting trot. Moonrock's action was shortlegged and active, so bumpy, and rising trot was easier on his rider. She had improved her rising trot considerably – instead of pushing herself up and down from her stirrups, she had copied other Dore Hill riders and now pushed her hips forward from the knees while rising. Pupils in her riding school had not been encouraged to sit to the trot, so the girl made herself ride without stirrups for a deeper seat.

On Saturday Madeline devoted time to plaiting. Standing on a box again, she wet the mane as prescribed by her book, then split the hairs into bunches – fortunately the book wasn't so old as to advise six big lumpy plaits and a seventh for the forelock. Moonrock sighed a deep heavy sigh, aware of what lay ahead for him.

"Mum," the girl had said that morning, "I need to plait."

"I thought you weren't showing?"

"No, it's for dressage. Apparently the judges won't look at you unless the horse is plaited."

"That doesn't seem fair. Surely they should be judging your riding and movement, not hairstyles?"

"I can't help it. I need a needle and strong thread, please."

"Are you plaiting in a stable? I suggest two needles. A good size – darning needle perhaps. That way you can thread it quickly and hold it securely. Any colour thread?"

"Grey or black?"

The hair was easier to plait when wet but only a few plaits had been sewn before the rest of the mane had dried off again, so the girl just kept water and brush beside her to wet as required. She could have experimented with elastic bands, but as she wanted the plaits to stay in place overnight she guessed that thread would prove more secure. The needle and scissors had to be juggled, and she found that the swiftest method was to tuck the scissors and spool into her jeans pocket, then to push her needle in and out of her old sweatshirt to keep it safe while she cut and knotted the thread. The water made her hands slippery but she managed not to lose the needle. The work took ages and she was grateful for her music.

Gary had gone shopping with his parents and now he returned, peering over the door to see Moonrock smartly plaited, with Madeline just snipping off the last thread in the forelock.

"Well done," he remarked. "Poor old boy, all this fussing. He doesn't look like himself – though you've made a great job of it. Was he good?"

"Stood like a rock," she assured him, switching off the music and removing her earbuds. "I think he even dropped off to sleep – he woke up and gave a little start!" She rewarded the cob with an apple. Moonrock stretched his neck down and shook it several times, but the neat little knobs of hair stayed in place.

"Don't dare roll," Gary ordered. "Come in for a cup of tea, Madeline, Mum bought you some cream cakes."

Niall read the newsletter and turned away from the e-mail impatiently. "Dressige," he complained. "Equitation. Sissy stuff. Imagine plaiting Tigger – he'd die laughing!"

Madeline was in a flurry of nerves, not aided by donning Caroline's black jacket and white tie. Gary stepped back to admire her when she appeared.

"Wow!"

"Is it okay?"

"Sensational. I've made your entry, and guess what? You're the only entrant for Primary."

"I can't be."

"Many people are influenced by the word 'test'. So do your best, smile and enjoy the round. You've already won, unless you fall off."

Much to her relief, the girl was able to remember the entire test and Moonrock behaved. Afterwards she dutifully divested herself of the borrowed jacket.

"Who are all these people? I don't see them normally at shows."

"Amazing," said Gary dryly, "how the prospect of Ballsbridge brings them out of the woodwork." Four-wheel drive vehicles had sprouted like mushrooms, and more than a dozen riders warmed up horses. Several were eventing riders who took dressage as a matter of course. By contrast many of the faithful weekly competitors didn't bother to attend, knowing that they would be outclassed.

Gary advised Madeline to watch and learn. Her scoresheet made her the winner, but was difficult to decipher. Four out of ten, why? Seven out of ten, why? Did anyone ever get ten out of ten? 'Incorrect bend,' the judge had written. 'Horse not sufficiently together.' Moonrock had been going forward willingly; she didn't know any way to improve.

"There's that Karen, with a green rosette," she pointed out. "She rode a very classy test."

"She seems to have been working hard on that mare," diagnosed Gary. The girl hoped that people would say something complimentary about herself.

Jen was unplaced because Dirk, new to the game, had been looking around rather than keeping his mind on his work. The equitation jumping commenced in the main arena. A simple course of eight fences had been constructed and each rider had to work on the flat for one minute, showing paces and turns, before jumping.

"See that girl," commented Gary, "she thinks she's doing well because she won at dressage. She's riding exactly the same way here. But does she look ready to jump? She's down in the saddle with long straight legs; she's leaning backwards and doing sitting trot; her horse is practically counting his footsteps and his head is near his knees." The bell rang and the pair cantered smoothly towards the first fence. The horse all but fell over it and barely managed to leave the poles intact.

"Not his fault," remarked Gary. "He didn't know he was in there to jump." Madeline could see what he meant – the girl's position was hindering the horse and she was left behind, hanging onto the reins, over every jump.

Karen trotted into the arena next and saluted the judges. She had shortened her leathers from dressage length so that her knees were slightly bent into the kneeroll of her saddle. Alabama had practice-jumped well and felt full of life, head raised but on the bit, hocks working under her as she prepared for fences. She made lovely circles and a trot serpentine, cantered a figure of eight with a short simple change of leg. Karen had reckoned that they were bound to mess up a flying change. The bell rang and she tapped the mare's shoulder with her whip, in warning. Alabama's ears pricked and she took the first fence in fine style.

"Very good," was Gary's comment as he watched the chestnut mare jump smoothly around, finding the correct leg for every turn, arcing over the centre of each obstacle. Karen rose with her back straight, head up and hands forward, all without looking forced or self-conscious. Only at the last fence did their concentration lapse; this happened to be a fan shape, which the mare hadn't seen before, and she got too close to the straight side and tapped it with her knees. The pole lifted up out of the cup and fell.

"Bad luck," said Gary. There was no announcement of faults and Madeline gathered that a clear was not the most important requirement. The next rider though, had two refusals, which Gary considered would be penalised severely.

Jen rode a good round on Dirk, once making a circle when she found that her turn hadn't left her young horse sufficient room to approach his fence. The grey knocked one pole.

"Of course I know I haven't a chance," Jen told Karen, grinning as she patted her grey's neck. "But I'd hate to miss the competition."

That evening Karen kissed her mother's cheek fondly and presented her with a third-place rosette and a fourth.

"Well done dear. Very good. Ahem... Mrs Foster remarked that she hadn't seen you playing pitch and putt this summer. Darling, it's good to see you so keen on your horse, but we don't want you turning into one of those horsey bores, do we? Maybe you'd spread your interests around a little more."

"If you insist Mum."

"Not that I insist, dear, and I do like to see hard work rewarded. Just keep it in mind. Now what did you win these for?"

"Dressage and equitation jumping. Mum, if I keep up this standard, there's a good chance that I may be sent to the RDS. The club sends a team of the best four in equitation, and so far I'm third."

"The Royal Dublin Society?" Mrs Langourne stared at her daughter, then at the rosettes. "You could really jump there?"

"Autumn, Mum, the National Championships."

CHAPTER ELEVEN

"There's a showing class in this schedule," noted Karen, "but I don't think Alabama would look right."

"She shouldn't show again this summer," Jen informed her bluntly. "She's fit as could be but not overweight like the judges want to see."

"What do professional show people do?"

"Feed stud nuts and conditioners," mused Jen. "Of course they might only show five or six times all summer. Often the horses get a couple of hours grazing each day – then the horses puff and sweat if they're unfit."

"So would I," chuckled Karen. She felt fitter now than she'd ever been, and was slim and agile without dieting in the slightest. Her mother, who struggled to control her weight, secretly envied the girl's carefree eating and if she had a lunch appointment, permitted herself no breakfast.

"Run a stables," said Jen with a grimace, "and you'll never have time to put on weight. Whatever calories I take don't get a chance to catch up on me." The two girls picked up brushes and went to start grooming.

"Got a letter from my sister," Jen mentioned. "She's worked her way over to San Francisco now; seeing all the sights and working as a waitress in all the Irish bars."

"It must be marvellous," sighed Karen. "Would you do it?"

"I couldn't leave the horses," said Jen automatically, then laughed. "I'd probably work my way around as a groom anyway."

Later Jen showed Karen how to rub petroleum jelly on the smooth skin under the mare's tail, and between her legs around her udder, to stop the skin drying and chapping. At her suggestion, instead of schooling that day, Karen affixed a long lead rein to Alabama's halter and took her out for a walk. They covered a couple of miles at a steady pace, learning about roads and gates and bicycles, pausing to browse on inviting verges, both of them thoroughly enjoying the break from normality. The mare tended to spook at dogs, probably because there were none in Shay's yard. On their way back, they called in to Karen's house.

"Mum, are you home?" The car filled the driveway. "Mum, here's Alabama." The chestnut was looking interestedly around, sniffing a rosebush.

"Karen, what on earth?" Mrs Langourne emerged from the front door. "Is something wrong?"

"No – I was walking her out and thought I'd let you see her."

"Oh. Quite handsome, isn't she? Does she eat roses? Do try not to let her leave hoofmarks on the lawn. Isn't she tall! Will she grow any bigger?"

Karen answered as best she could, until the mare took a snatch at a tasty shrub. Her mother stifled a protest, but the girl judged it wiser to depart. Just in case the bush wasn't safe to eat, she picked a few leaves and showed them to Jen back at the yard.

"Contorted hazel, Mum's favourite. It's not poisonous is it?"

"Hazel is safe enough. So are roses. The ones to watch for are yew, rhododendron, privet, box, anything with a thick shiny leaf like laurel; laburnum, rhubarb leaves, also hemlock, henbane, hogweed, ragwort. Can you recognise all those?"

"I don't think so."

"Find pictures of them on line; search them out in hedges or garden centres until you do know them all. If in doubt don't let her eat."

Jen was such a mine of information, but she didn't come across as a know-all. Her practical help taught Karen something every day, and the younger girl willingly lent a hand with work.

Niall attended the next Dore Hill show, because as well as the dressage and equitation, there was to be a Top Score and Gamblers' Stakes. Novice riders took part in Top Score, aiming to accumulate points for each fence they managed to jump within a time limit. Tigger won this class handsomely, building up an unassailable total, and Madeline came third, to her surprise. The larger fences carried more points, and as the riders could choose their own line and jump a fence twice if they had time, the girl had selected the higher scoring jumps. Niall came to chat with her as they watched the thrilling Gamblers' Stakes. Madeline thought that it was nice to see Niall again. She was glad he had noticed the progress she was making.

For Open riders, a tall joker fence sat in the middle of the arena. The course builder had made this a plank fence, built of only two planks with no groundline. Each fence scored from 30 points (a crosspole) through 60 (a spread) to 150 (a high, wide parallel) and all could be jumped from either direction – no triple bar or fan, but hogsbacks, verticals and parallels. The joker carried 200 points. If that fence fell, too bad, the score was reduced by 200. Quite a few people finished laughing, with a minus score. The winner cleared the joker once and took no further risk, concentrating on high scoring fences.

Karen did well, as Alabama had learnt to clear fences carefully and they managed the joker once, but they weren't fast enough at accumulating points to do better than fourth place. Jen didn't bother with the Gamblers' but was satisfied with the day's other results.

Gary wandered over to talk to the secretary, and he was quietly asked if Madeline would consider upgrading.

"I'm sure she'd love it, but is she ready?"

"She's doing really well," pointed out Mrs Conroy. "The other Primary riders will start to glare at her soon. They are a lot more beginnerish."

"Probably," acknowledged Gary.

"We need a team quickly. Our own Inter-Club fixture is two weeks away, and the Regional day is just afterwards. Everyone must pull together if we are to win the Challenge Shield."

Hannah Brooks frowned at Karen, who was unsaddling Alabama.

"Mare's coming on now for you, isn't she? Mind, she looks very fit."

"She is," returned Karen, wondering why the woman didn't sound approving. Jen had heard and explained quietly later.

"If people say your horse looks fit, that's a polite way of saying thin. The opposite is to say a horse looks well, or like a hunter – that's overweight. Don't pay any attention. Alabama's building up so much muscle that she has nothing to spare for fat. She's being wormed, she's getting as much feed as she'll eat and a conditioner too. That woman just likes to criticise. See, she's gone over to Maire with that fat slob of a horse – probably telling her he looks extremely well!"

Shay was bandaging Cootehill Lad's tail for travelling, since he tended to lean back against the rear of the box.

"You did well, Hugh," he praised the retired man who was leading his older horse past, having come third.

"Bit of fun," said Hugh, smiling. "I actually worried that someone might raise an objection to old Joker here, since he has a higher grade, and the class was based on speed, so I mentioned this to the judges. The next thing I hear an announcement. 'This class is confined to members of the Dore Hill

Riding Club. If anyone has an objection to any other competitor, this should be lodged in writing with the judges before the start, accompanied by a fifty euro deposit. Any objection deemed to be frivolous will forfeit the deposit.'"

The little group laughed.

"I could fix you up with a grand young horse," offered Shay.

"I wouldn't trust a young horse, not at my time of life," returned Hugh. "And I couldn't feed two, so Joker it is, as long as he's happy."

"He's in top form," agreed Shay. "With a gloss on his coat."

"That's right. And it didn't come out of a bottle either."

"Madeline," said Gary as they drove home, "the selection committee would like you to consider moving up a grade for jumping classes. If you did that, they could put you on a team – they are short of Intermediates, and Moonrock is tried and trusted."

"A team?" the girl repeated, looking almost scared.

"Nobody's insisting," he assured her. "And I said it must be your choice entirely because you haven't much experience. But for what it's worth, I believe you have the ability."

"Wow!" Excitement coloured her voice. "Wait'll I tell mum and dad – and Eamonn!"

Niall was asked to be a team member, which pleased him until he realised that the B team was intended. He rode home unsure whether he had been snubbed or honoured. If the selectors thought highly enough of him to put him on a team, why not the best team? He'd probably have to put up with pathetic team mates. He'd have no chance with that townie girl Madeline for instance. Someone had said she might get asked to upgrade. She was only a Primary.

"Everyone has to take turns," commented his mother reasonably over dinner.

"Tigger's the greatest," defended his younger brother stoutly.

"Perhaps they need a top-class novice on the B team," considered his father, "so a weaker person's score can be dropped. A team is only as strong as the weakest member. Niall, less of your complaints, lad; make sure your score isn't the one that has to be dropped."

Shay good-humouredly accepted the task of being captain.

"B team? Doesn't matter to me," he said with a shrug. "I'll just be concentrating on clear rounds no matter what the others do. Don't expect a fast round against the clock – if we get that far. But sometimes a steady clear can win the day."

"By the way," asked the chairman, "how is that girl Karen getting on?"

"Doing fine," asserted Shay, "you can see that for yourself. Improving with every show. She's plugging in a lot of hard work at my place... quite a transformation from when she rode a pony."

"Mum," sighed Madeline, "I really don't know if I should go up a grade. I mean, there's so much to learn."

"But you'll keep on learning," her mother told her as they washed and dried the dishes. "You'd be like second year in school – not ready to sit the final leaving exams. How will you learn except by progressing? You don't want to get bored."

"True."

"Didn't you tell us you jumped against all the Intermediates the other day?"

"Oh yes, in the Top Score. I jumped the same fences."

"Then I don't expect you'd have any problems. After all you've been riding for years. If you really don't feel ready, don't upgrade. But if you look at it as a challenge?"

At the end of the week Gary rang Mrs Conroy to tell her that Madeline was upgrading and would be available for team selection.

CHAPTER TWELVE

With no show that weekend at Dore Hill, Karen, Jen and Shay went to a small SJAI show. Jen wasn't riding because Dirk wasn't registered. Shay's young horse jumped high and clear, and an interested party afterwards remarked that the gelding showed promise as an eventer.

"A winter's hunting and a spring's hunter trials," agreed Shay, "and he'll win events for you."

"Maybe in a month or two I'll come back to you."

Alabama gazed all around her because the surroundings were unfamiliar, but as she was Grade E the mare was allowed to walk the course, which was a great help. She jumped two clear rounds in the 0-15 points class, winning her first registered point.

"I think she's done enough for the day, has she?" asked Karen.

"Good, keep her happy," agreed Jen. "Don't forget to collect your winnings."

While prize money wasn't huge at this level, it was divided equally among the winners. The more double clears, the less money each received.

"Congratulations," praised Shay. "On getting paid that is. Some shows send on cheques months later. Some shows forget." He pocketed his own winnings; it would help cover entries and diesel. Shows which paid out on the day were immensely popular.

The three watched the other events, Jen and Shay being acquainted with most of the riders.

"Might get your name in the paper for that win," Shay remarked to Karen.

"Really?" She looked anxiously to see if he was teasing.

"Not the daily," he temporised. "The *Irish Field* or the *Farmers' Journal*. The local paper too. They don't always have room but it's worth a look."

Mrs Langourne was suitably pleased with Karen's win, but a rosette wasn't much and one couldn't place a few euros on a shelf.

"Now that you're winning, you clever girl, I wonder if there are any handsome trophies that you could snap up? Lucinda does so promote her daughter's swimming talents, and it would be so nice to let her see, next bridge meeting, that you are achieving with your horse already. I wouldn't boast, naturally, but a fine trophy speaks for itself."

Niall practised after tea in the long bright evenings, not raising the fences but making the spreads wider and removing the groundlines from the verticals. He altered strides between fences so that the pony had to look properly at each fence and clear it with care. Niall built doubles and trebles, Tigger's weak spot as he had a short stride, and made sure to keep them both balanced between obstacles and keep his weight off the pony's forehand. He built narrow fences to mimic a stile. Tigger became foot perfect.

Madeline also put in extra work, since Gary had decided to paint his poles and barrels. He drove to the local hardware.

"Have you any secondhand paint?" he asked, and the proprietor roared with laughter. Once he had divined what was required he produced several battered tins, unopened, of various sizes and colours. Gary got the lot at a bargain price with a few cheap paintbrushes. He and Madeline slapped paint on everything, transforming the fences and helping to preserve the wood. With a surplus of white, they painted three poles white all over, which looked extremely well as a fan, vertical or triple bar.

"I never realised how rusty the barrels had become," commented the girl.

"Neighbours don't like looking out at junk," Gary told her. "Horse owners should keep standards up. You never know when the Tidy Towns inspectors will drive by, either. You'll enjoy jumping these fences now!" Speckles of white decorated his hair and old shirt and jeans. Madeline's father had given her one of his old shirts which she'd donned over her clothes, keeping them clean. True enough, the fences did look new and inviting. That evening Moonrock snorted warily and jumped higher than usual over the fences.

"They get careless and bored, jumping the same old things all the time," Gory observed. "Ever jumped a treble? I'm not sure, but you might get one at the Inter Club show."

Madeline had to admit that she hadn't.

"Don't worry, Moonrock has." He set up a treble with the distance between obstacles carefully paced.

"Concentrate on riding straight down the middle," he instructed. "Sit up slightly between elements, like a double, but make sure he has his head over each jump."

The girl found no problem as the cob knew the trick. Gary raised the poles slightly and Moonrock flew over the combination easily. Then Gary moved the last part further back, so Moonrock had to take a full stride on the ground, not just land and take off. Madeline had time to sit up straight and feel the reins before the last jump. She wanted to try again, but Gary said that this work was hard on a horse's joints and mustn't be overdone on rock-solid ground such as they now had – the farmers were alternately wishing for rain to make the grass grow and hoping that it would hold off until all the harvests were completed. Professional jumpers had sand arenas.

Watching Moonrock grazing after his work, Madeline's eyes were drawn to the bright fences.

"That's definitely smartened up the place," she said, smiling.

"Caroline helped me last time, for her to jump. Very sophisticated, she is now, on the Skype. Chatting all about the different types of wine and villages with swallows' nests and mansard roofs. And churches and galleries and museums."

"I'd like to visit France," said Madeline.

"I wouldn't," said Gary. "They eat horses there, you know."

Karen helped to wash numnahs, bandages, girths and rugs.

"Wonderful to get the weather to dry these rugs," exclaimed Jen. "They can take days." Too heavy for a line, the dripping gear had to be hung over a fence. With the amount of horses and ponies in the livery yard, and the frequency of shows, the washing built up until Jen got time and fair weather.

"I put the numnahs in my parents' washing machine once," she recalled when Karen wondered about the laborious hand washing in the tin bath. "They came out a treat, like new. But a week later we had to call the repair man. He found that the filter for the outflow pipe was choked with horses' hairs, which was why the machine had flooded our kitchen. I wasn't popular after that."

On Saturday Karen arrived at the stable in time to help Shay load two ponies which, with their riders, were going to a Pony Club camp.

"Those ponies will be lying down exhausted in their stables on Monday morning from the excitement," prophesied Jen. "Won't do them any harm." She assisted other youngsters to tack and mount, and saw them set out to the schooling field.

"No big jumps," she warned them. "And put down the chinstrap on your hat, Christy."

"Shay doesn't wear a hard hat," retorted the boy.

"If you don't wear that hat, and properly, you don't ride," threatened Jen. "And I'll tell your parents why." The boy subsided, glowering. "I'll be out to keep an eye on you three later," she added. "How about some mounted games? I'll bring buckets and flags and tennis balls." The kids radiated eagerness and set off happily.

"Anything I can do?" enquired Karen.

"You can read the *Field*."

Mrs Langourne did not favour the *Irish Field*, which was chiefly devoted to racehorses. But within the weekly paper was a section called *Irish Horse World* which covered everything from Connemaras to Irish Draughts, Ballinasloe horse fair to eventing, dressage, driving, equestrian weddings and deaths, hunting, polo and showjumping.

Unable to believe the implicit message, Karen went to the tackroom and picked up the *Field*. Thumbing through the pages she read the results columns. Dressage in the north, pony shows in the west, jumping in the south, polo in the Phoenix Park, Dublin. Then she spotted the name of the small show at which she'd won.

"Grade E, 0 – 15 points. There I am right beside S. Broughton – Cootehill Lad. K. Langourne - Alabama." She stared, unable to absorb the words. Everyone in the country could read this result.

"Sure the print won't fade with all that reading?" asked Jen with a grin. "You can keep that," she offered. "I wouldn't be surprised if it makes a difference at Dore Hill too."

"What kind of difference?" wondered Karen. But Jen would say no more, and got on with her tasks.

CHAPTER THIRTEEN

Madeline was helping her mother and Eamonn with grocery shopping one afternoon, in the large supermarket and cluster of shops just outside the town centre. They'd paid at the checkout and were pushing a trolley of goods to the door, chatting about tacos and how to make them, since Eamonn had asked to have them for dinner. Madeline spotted Janey Coughlan off to one side, and was about to wave when she realised that the other girl was surrounded by three store staff. A lady in a dark skirt and jacket had Janey by the arm and the manageress was talking sternly; the security guard who staffed the camera screen, usually a boring job, stood beside them with a few small but high-value items on his desk. Perfume, face cream, a phone handset.

"Our store policy is always to prosecute," the family group heard the manageress explain. "You need to contact your parents; we've already sent for the Guards."

"Oh," breathed Madeline, stricken with horror.

"Shush," said her mother and waited to talk until they were in the car park. "I knew that brassie would come to no good," she said then with a sigh.

"Is that big trouble?" Eamonn wanted to know. His eyes were round.

"Yes it is. This doesn't look like a case of eating sweets as you shop and forgetting to pay for them.

Janey may be let off in court with a caution as she's so young but everyone in town will know."

"She's not bad," said Madeline. "She just doesn't have anything else to do. And her parents don't have jobs so she can't afford to buy what she wants."

"That's not our business," her mother reminded her. "Have you been in contact with her since I gave you back your phone?"

"No. I actually forgot about her, I was so busy."

"Just as well."

Dore Hill's grounds were indicated with posters on telephone poles and signposts, for the benefit of visiting clubs. On the day four other clubs sent teams and individuals.

"All getting ready for next weekend," commented Niall to two of his brothers, who had attended on their bikes. "Next week's a big event, see, the whole Region's clubs are putting teams together."

The newsletter had requested each member to bring some item of food or drink, for a party after the jumping. Home-made food was greatly appreciated, Gary had hinted, and Madeline had given her best efforts to producing a coffee sponge cake, which travelled with care in a round biscuit tin. This attracted many compliments when she proffered it to the committee. Gary had imperturbably agreed to provide something he'd made himself; however what emerged was a packet of crackers and a box of several cheeses, sliced by Gary's own hand.

Everything was welcome. Niall handed in chocolate biscuits and a carton of orange juice; Karen had been busy baking, and went to donate her pie to the feast before it was squashed. Home economics was taught in boarding school.

"Oh Karen," Mrs Conroy greeted her, "glad you came."

"Yes? Here's an apple tart, I hope that's okay. I made it with cinnamon."

"Wonderful, thanks. It does look good, I fancy a slice later. Would you like to jump on a team today?"

"Me? Really?"

"You've been a good supporter and improving steadily, so we thought you might like a place on the B team."

"Would I have to go against the clock? We haven't done that yet."

"No, the captain would – Shay. If you did have a bad round, they could always discard your score. But I'm sure you'll be fine."

Karen agreed, her head spinning.

The vice-chairman strolled over to Gary and Madeline as they set out to walk the course for the individual event.

"Good day, folks... looks like a large crowd. We'd like to have a good chance in the team event, so we definitely need two teams. Would you jump on the B team, Madeline, since you've upgraded?"

"Yes please! Who else is on it?"

"Shay Broughton is captain. Niall Johnson is a novice and we're arranging the other Open."

"Two good ones anyway," said Gary, nodding. "And Madeline and Moonrock won't let you down."

"Better not let you down either," chuckled the official, "or I imagine they'll walk home."

Individual competitions were jumped first, beginning with Primary. Only a couple of Primary riders had come from other clubs, as they could not make up teams. With only six in the class it was over quickly.

"Not riding today, Madeline?" called a Dore Hill Primary rider.

"I am," she replied. "Intermediate."

"That's telling 'em," Gary agreed quietly. "Up you get, and check your girth." The girl mounted, found her stirrups without looking as she gathered her reins, and walked on, feeling the tension on the girth as she rode.

The course consisted of ten fences, but no treble. There were two doubles and the second would be made into a treble for the Opens. Madeline discovered that the fences were slightly higher than Primary, but she'd been jumping this height at home. She rode her first round with great determination and was thrilled to be clear. The next competitor, a girl with Millford RC on her saddlecloth, looked pale and nervous.

"Good luck," Madeline said impulsively as they passed each other at the pocket. The girl gave her a watery smile. She had three refusals at the first fence and trotted out hanging her head. Madeline had been watching.

"Are you all right?" she had to ask as the girl slipped off her plain-faced brown cob.

"I feel terrible," sighed the Millford girl. "I've been so nervous, I haven't eaten for two days. I never went to an Inter-club before; and I just knew Bobby wouldn't jump strange fences. He's only used to Millford Lodge – that's where I get lessons. He's a school horse and I hired him for the day."

"Are you on a team later?"

"Yes… and now I'll get them eliminated."

"Oh no, you won't," Madeline returned. "They only need three scores to finish; if you have a bad round, let them all get on with it."

"Really?"

"Sure. There are dozens in this class… would you like a cup of tea? I'm having one anyway, here's Gary with the cups."

Gary obligingly gave the girls the tea and went to get more for himself. Niamh, dark–haired and pale-skinned, calmed down sufficiently to sip her tea and discuss her horse.

"What can I try to get him moving?"

"Stick of dynamite," prescribed Gary. "How old is he?"

"I've no idea."

"Getting on a bit, I imagine, from the depths of the hollows above his eyes and – open up, Bobby – the length of his teeth. Did you choose him?"

"Well," considered Niamh, "everyone else had made their arrangements and Bobby was the only horse left that wasn't a pony, when they asked me to come too. I mean, he'd never throw anyone and he's very good with beginners, he doesn't mind if they pull the reins or slip. So I do like him." Bobby was grazing, unconcerned, and rubbing his eye on his knee to get rid of flies.

"I should say he's happier back there," said Gary. "Don't tire him out in the practise ring and he might jump better later."

When the round finished and the course was raised, Madeline and the other clear riders jumped a second round. Six of them had double clears.

"Well done, all of you," the judge told the riders over the loudspeaker. "We have trophies for first, second and third places. We've been timing you and found an average time taken by all the clear riders in the last round. We'll ask you six to jump again and the best round closest to the average time, which we won't disclose yet, will win. Second will be the next closest, whether faster or slower. You're not to hurry – but try to go clear."

Madeline saw Niall getting ready for his class and anxiously asked him for hints.

"You ride at a good steady pace," he considered. "Don't push him or you'll definitely be too fast – some of those were real slowcoaches. If you think you're too fast, ride wider on the turns. Make sure to go clear – someone's bound to have faults."

The judges drew for the order of jumping; three riders were from Dore Hill. Madeline was fourth to ride. Gary wished her luck. The first horse went clear, the second knocked a pole. Third, clear. Madeline felt her heart pounding as she rode forward into the arena.

"Madeline Kelly riding Moonrocket for Dore Hill." The cob gave a little squeal when she tapped him on the shoulder with her whip. He pranced, looking for his first fence. The bell sounded, and they were off – rather quickly. After the first fence Moonrock set out in a gallop and the girl desperately tried to slow him. As the next upright loomed closer, all she could do was ride for the fence, and they were clear. Recalling Niall's advice she rode a long turn as Moonrock was pulling on the snaffle. They finished without incurring faults. The judge was timing each round with a stopwatch.

"Whew, what happened there?" the bewildered Madeline asked Gary.

"He thought he was to go for a speed round. He did plenty with me and if you felt tense he'd pick that up... probably wondered why you were holding him back!"

"Niall suggested I ride wide turns."

"I was nervous," said Gary sheepishly. "I didn't want to watch."

The next horse had four faults and the final one was clear in a slow time. After several moments' calculations, the judges disclosed the placings.

Madeline came third. The hidden time was revealed, and she had been three seconds faster.

"Well done," called Hugh Roe as he helped to raise the course. "Just don't try so hard next time!"

"Not bad out of such a big entry," commented Shay. "Rest him before the next class, please!"

Prizes would be awarded at the end of the day. Moonrock was untacked, put back in his box after a few minutes' grazing, and left to rest.

Niall jumped effortlessly clear through two rounds and was drawn first – worst - against the clock. He pulled out all the stops, trying to set the others an unbeatable target. Turning on a sixpence into the final planks, Tigger had insufficient room to jump. A less brave horse would have refused, but the dun pony folded up his legs somehow and buckled his back to give himself height without spread. Niall gripped with his knees as they leapt at an angle across the fence. He knew he was close to one wing, but didn't realise how close until his knee and toe brushed the upright. His toe must have been sticking out and caught the wing, rocking it; that was enough to send the plank crashing off its flat cup.

Tigger hared through the finish, past the two official timekeepers thumbing stopwatches, but the dreaded "four faults" sounded ominously. Dejected, Niall trotted back to the pocket, where he patted Tigger and fed him mints, assuring the pony that he hadn't been to blame. Four other riders waited tensely to jump. One galloped flat-out around all the corners, and had two poles down. Another tried the same sharp turn into the planks as Niall had, and the larger horse refused. He cleared the plank on a wider approach, gaining three faults. The next horse sauntered around, making no effort to go fast, gaining a slow clear. The last horse moved more quickly but took no chances, and was clear. Niall was fourth.

"Don't know why we bothered," he grumbled to the other Dore Hill riders; by the luck of the draw, all the visiting competitors had been drawn after them and had known what they had to beat.

Open riders were allowed to walk the course while it was being adjusted; a double become a treble, spreads were widened and top poles raised. Extra fillers such as straw bales and birch hurdles were brought in to make the taller fences appear more solid.

The Open riders were far more businesslike than the novices, especially around the practise jump. A steward had to ensure that the obstacle was not raised too high or wide, nor erected as a spread with the back bar below the height of the front. Sometimes riders would purposely do this to make the horse work harder, but it could cause accidents. They would never admit to doing this, but would claim that the fence had mistakenly been built in that fashion.

Karen and Shay rode loosely around the pocket, then began to trot and canter, asking their horses to flex their plaited, gleaming necks. Visiting riders cast glances at them, noting their immaculate turnouts and the professional tack. Shay jumped clear without fuss; Alabama was feeling full of oats and gave her rider a few hairy moments, but incurred no faults. Karen wished Jen was with her, but the blonde girl had a yard to run. The chestnut mare squealed and kicked, or switched her tail, if another horse came near, so that Karen had to say "Young horse, keep clear," continually.

"She's not normally a kicker," worried Karen. "Or I'd have put a red ribbon on her tail."

"Showing people never do that," Shay corrected her. "Nor jumping people. Why bring down the value of your horse? Any young horse might kick. She might be a bit hot today." Translated this meant that Alabama might be coming into season, when mares are notoriously unpredictable.

The second round was over a shorter course, but raised. Karen and Shay both jumped clear; so did a visiting rider and Fiona Conroy. In the third round, Cootehill Lad made a nice stylish clear, his rider not putting him under any pressure. The visitor turned out a spectacular clear round, fast enough to scare Karen into a steady clear, with Fiona taking up the challenge for the home side, scraping the poles as she turned in mid-air and booting on for home after the last. She came in half a second ahead and the crowd cheered delightedly.

Individual events completed, the course builders adjusted the course, changing numbers and reversing some obstacles. Shay, as team captain, gathered his team mates and walked the course with them, warning of awkward spots and pacing the distances. Karen listened carefully and Niall paid attention, but Madeline was so excited she could hardly remember the fences, let alone the strides.

"So far so good," commented one of the Johnson boys as Niall completed a clear round. Madeline had already managed a clear. The course was suitable for novice jumpers and all grades would jump it twice. The teams had been drawn in order of competing, and when Dore Hill B's turn came again Karen entered the ring, waited for the bell and commenced her round. Alabama tapped the first fence with her knees and the pole fell. Karen couldn't believe it and continued with extra care, incurring no more faults.

"Hard luck," commiserated Niall. "Could happen to anyone."

Karen felt distressed. Even Maire had achieved a clear for the A team.

"Don't worry," Niall reassured her kindly, "we can discard your score if Shay goes clear."

"It's only four anyway," added Madeline, encouraged to talk to the red-haired girl. "And she has a fantastic jump most times."

Shay was warming up and frowned. "He doesn't feel very keen," he muttered to Karen. In the ring Cootehill Lad started slowly and made an awkward jump over the first. He seemed reluctant to approach the second fence.

"What's wrong?" Madeline asked Karen.

"I don't know," Karen could only rely.

Cootehill Lad cleared the second fence from a cat-jump, as he'd come too close to take off properly but Shay's legs had forced him forward. Then he stuck his heavy head up in the air and sideways, jaw firm, and refused to turn for the third. Shay had to spend a minute sorting him out and getting his head down again before the horse ungraciously agreed to complete his round. The judge gave him three faults for resistance.

"Damn the brute," growled Shay as he rejoined his team mates. He so seldom expressed anger that Karen realised just how furious he was; the gelding had a surly expression with laid-back ears, flaring nostrils and white rimmed eyes. He chomped on the bit. "Just grabbed the bit and crossed his jaw somehow – seemed to feel he'd done enough for the day." The man dismounted and led the gelding around the pocket. "Might have a cramp – or a touch of colic or azoturia – nothing wrong with his legs. I'll see how he settles and whether he shows signs of problems, maybe change his bit and noseband." The man took off his hard hat and wiped his high forehead. "I'm sorry folks, it's bad for the team. But at least I got him around."

Shay's three faults was the final score for the B team in that round, discarding Karen's four. The A team smirked with a clean sheet, and the other two teams were clear after discards. In the second round the newly confident Madeline, relieved that the two Opens had faulted instead of her, managed another clear, and Niall did likewise.

"That Tigger really hates hitting poles," complimented Karen. Niall flashed her a grin, thinking that she was much more normal than her turnout would suggest.

Alabama was tiring by now and went obediently into the ring, neck bowed and ears pricked. She knew the course and made no mistakes, just clearing each fence by a small amount. Karen sensed that the mare was trying her best and put no pressure on her, only tapping her shoulder with the whip as they turned for the final fence. Alabama stood off and picked up her knees in response, and they finished with a clear, to the cheers of the home crowd.

"Well done, Karen," cried Maire, who had been unplaced in the individual event. Karen was beaming as she slipped off her breathless mare and slackened her girths. Alabama had finished work now, and deserved a rest. Madeline came up shyly, having put Moonrock in his trailer, and offered Karen an apple for the chestnut mare.

"Thank you – she'll love that," said the Open rider, blushing with pleasure. "Is Shay ready?"

"He's not going. Niall says Shay doesn't have to ride because we have three clears so we can't improve the score. If need be he'll go against the clock."

"I'm not used to teams," apologised Karen.

"Neither am I," confessed Madeline.

"Weren't you a Primary?"

"I was, but everyone said I might as well be Intermediate since the club needed team members, and I thought I'd go for it."

"You did extremely well," praised Karen. "I expect they'll put you on the A team next time."

"Not likely – they all went clear. Their captain's ready to jump off – one other team is all clear so far." Competing early, she had been able to keep track of the scores. "Shall I help you put Alabama away? What a beautiful face she has – very dainty."

The mare had sweated under her bridle and turned to rub her itchy face against Karen. Careful of her jacket, the girl scratched her fondly. Madeline was glad she'd taken off her borrowed black jacket.

Shay's services were not required because Dore Hill A and Clansha teams drew on double clears after discards; in a tense jump-off they fought it out and each rider knocked one pole but their times were close. Clansha were first and Fiona Conroy, captain of the A team, took second place. Breamont Club finished equal third with Dore Hill B and behind them was Millford, which had totalled eighteen faults in the first round and twelve in the second despite discards. One team had been eliminated as one rider had taken a wrong course and another had had three refusals.

Everyone gathered for the prizegiving, torn between the table of glittering trophies, silver and green Connemara marble, and colourful rosettes, and the other tables laden with tempting food and drink.

The Primary riders received their awards first, then the Intermediates. Madeline felt so proud to have gained a prize in her higher grade, and the large yellow and white rosette, with a bronze medal depicting a horse's head, fully justified her decision. In Niall's class the visitors had taken the honours. His partisan brothers refused to clap, though Niall set a good example. The Open marble trophy went to Fiona Conroy and Karen was third, ahead of Shay, and blushed to the roots of her hair as she collected her ribbon and medal.

Next the team prizes were awarded, and since Braemount A and Dore Hill B were equal third, the two captains were asked to pick a rosette from a riding hat held above their heads. To the home side's delight Shay drew the yellow and they collected third-place prizes while Braemount took the green rosettes for fourth. Karen and Madeline, lining up with the others for photos, looked at each other and laughed.

"I never knew Alabama could go so well," said Karen.

"Moonrock didn't touch a single pole, he's a real champion."

"How's your horse, Shay?" enquired Niall after taking a selfie on his phone, showing himself between the two girls. They were decent looking girls, all the same, he'd been thinking, might as well put this shot up on his social page. No need to add to the page that one of them was a right townie and into rock music, and the other was the developer's daughter.

"Seems quite normal," said Shay with a frown. "No reason for his jibbing that I can find. He might have had a slight cramp or something."

"Mule-headed," was Jen's scathing opinion when she heard of the incident.

CHAPTER FOURTEEN

During the next week Moonrock got a good rest from jumping. He also received a worm dose, which he disliked intensely. Gary put a hand on Moonrock's grey nose and worked the large plastic syringe into the corner of the cob's mouth where there were no teeth. He pushed the paste out onto the cob's tongue, holding his jaws firmly closed to stop him from spitting out the dose. After a minute Moonrock swallowed and Gary released him. The two people stood back, amused, as the cob opened his mouth and shook his head, rolling his eyes in disgust.

"How often does he get that?" Madeline asked.

"Some people dose every eight weeks," replied Gary. "Moonrock gets his once a quarter – he never looks thin. It's better to alternate brands in case the worms become immune to one. I give him a day or two off work after dosing."

Niall had no time to ride Tigger, for he was busy on the farm.

Karen rested Alabama and assisted Jen to school Dirk. The blonde girl rode up a gradual slope onto a small bank, and when the grey looked dubiously at the steep side he was being asked to descend, Karen attached a lead rope to his bit and encouraged him to follow her down the slope. The iron grey soon became keen on this activity and jumped up and down with the barest urging from his rider. There was a small trench, six feet long and only three feet wide, at the top of the schooling field, and the girls had built a spread fence over this, concealing the hole with thick brush in front and using long poles as wings. Dirk jumped the low inviting spread readily, not realising that a ditch lay underneath, and by the time he came around to jump it again Karen had pulled away some brush so that the hole showed through patches.

The grey looked hard at this fence, but the rest of the obstacle was familiar so he leapt way up in the air, peering down with a free head, and made a big arc above the fence to ensure that he wasn't going to land in a hole. Jen patted him and assured him that he was brave, and he decided that ditches were not so scary.

"You're a fantastic rider," said Karen. "You sit so tight and never get left behind or pull his mouth. They always jump well for you."

"That's what training youngsters does for you," said Jen self-consciously. "Anyone can sit on an armchair."

Shay tacked Cootehill Lad on Friday morning, when he had a spare hour. The big horse felt stiff but soon loosened up as he went through schooling figures in the dressage arena. Dore Hill had scheduled its final qualifiers of dressage and equitation for Saturday, so as not to conflict with Sunday's Inter-Club. Shay had been asked to captain a team again but his main effort would be towards qualifying for the RDS. Sunday's show would be useful in that his horse would gain experience in different surroundings. However the gelding had better behave himself... Shay had been unsettled by the horse's behaviour, though he hadn't wanted to admit it. Most horses would go on trying gamely to clear fences so the rider had to be aware of any lameness and pull up. Cootehill Lad had been sound.

Jen and Karen were teaching an unbroken pony to lunge at the bottom of the field. The pony persisted in stopping and turning, so Karen led him while Jen voiced encouragement from the centre of the circle. Short sessions were better than asking the youngster to concentrate for too long, so after twenty minutes they allowed the pony to graze.

"I ought really to be getting on with everything," reflected Jen, chewing sweet clover. "But you know, the work is always there no matter what; it seems a shame to ignore this beautiful day."

"Shay is too busy to tell us off," chuckled Karen. "He's jumping now."

"Some girls spend their school holidays working in shops or taking computer courses," said Jen. "Ever thought of that?"

"No way!" exclaimed Karen. "I want time off after boarding school – you get no time to yourself." Then they both realised that something was amiss.

Having jumped three or four fences without problem, Shay had turned his potential eventer towards the spread over the ditch. Cootehill Lad had not jumped this previously but managed to sense the trench under the brushwood. He came close enough to confirm his suspicion and jibbed abruptly. Shay sat firm and kicked hard; the horse reared. Shay instinctively encircled the horse's neck with his right arm, leaning forward, while the girls at the other end of the field watched tensely.

Most horses would have dropped down; possibly Cootehill Lad was wary of putting his feet in an unseen hole. He maintained his rear, shuffling his hind feet, and threw his big head sideways. Shay yelled into his ear, but the gelding ignored the noise and threw his head higher.

"Hold the pony," Jen directed, flinging the lunge rope at Karen and running. Long before she had neared Shay, the enormous brown gelding had overbalanced and fallen over backwards.

Karen screamed as Shay was lost under the horse's bulk. The pony whinnied nervously and she realised that she could do nothing with him in tow. Catching the rein nearer to the headcollar, she trotted him back to the yard and put him into his stable.

Shay must be all right – he must be.

Desperately she ran back across the yard, her heart pounding, and into the field. Cootehill Lad, riderless, stirrups flapping, trotted along the top hedge. Jen was bending over near the ditch jump, and as she saw Karen stood straight to wave. She motioned holding a telephone to her ear.

"Ambulance!" she cried, the urgency carrying across the open space. Karen turned and raced to the tackroom, grabbing her phone from her coat which was hanging on a hook. She dialled the emergency number 112 and asked for the ambulance, giving the address and her phone number when asked, explaining what had happened. Then she grabbed a light blanket from the tackroom and rushed out, praying as she ran that Shay was not too badly hurt.

"He's unconscious," Jen told her briefly. "Looks like rib damage."

"Ambulance is on the way," gasped Karen, handing over the blanket. Jen was afraid to move Shay in case of serious injuries, but she laid the blanket over him. His bald head was bleeding and the cloth cap lay nearby on the thin skin of grass covering the iron-hard ground.

"He's breathing, look. Scalp cuts always bleed a lot – it's probably minor," the older girl tried to reassure Karen. All they could do was wait.

CHAPTER FIFTEEN

Madeline had gained proficiency at plaiting and on Friday evening sewed in Moonrock's plaits with extra care, for she wanted them to last until Sunday. The cob had done no dressage during the week, to prevent boredom. Early on Saturday morning she groomed Moonrock as he munched his feed, then polished the tack and washed her riding boots. Gary backed the four-wheel drive over to the trailer.

"There'll be a slight delay, Madeline," he announced, poking his head into the tackroom. "We've a flat tyre – I never glanced at the trailer all week."

"Oh dear." The girl set aside her tack and came to help. Gary produced a star-shaped wheelbrace from the boot and loosened the trailer's wheel studs while Madeline, as directed, let down the little jack at the rear of the trailer. When the flat tyre began to lift off the ground she wound down the jockey-wheel at the front of the trailer, and lifted the two wheels on that side clear of the ground. Gary let her finish winding off the studs while he fetched the spare, which was mounted on the side wall. These were large, heavy wheels, with broad thick tyres; the girl pulled off the flat and Gary held the good one in place while she screwed on the studs.

"Just a minute," he said, and fetched a can of oil left from the last time he'd topped up his engine. Trickling oil down onto the dusty wheel bolts, he explained that this would make the studs easier to remove next time. Madeline wound the studs tight with the star brace, then Gary let down the jack, administering a final tightening to the studs by using his foot on the brace for extra strength.

"All done – thanks for your help!"

"Of course I'd help." Madeline sounded puzzled as she washed her dirty hands.

"Caroline wouldn't take that attitude," Gary compared them. "She'd say that changing wheels was for men."

"Why? Okay, they're heavy, but it's just something that has to be done."

"Better get on the road. We don't want to be late."

Madeline hurried across when they arrived at the competition field, because the nuisance of being the first dressage competitor was that the next competition might start if she didn't arrive on time. As it turned out another Primary rider had entered too.

"Are you free tomorrow, Madeline?" wondered Mrs Conroy. "We'd like to send you on a team again if you can travel."

"Wonderful! I'd love to go, I know that Gary will agree. Is it the same team as before?"

"Not quite." The woman frowned. "I'm afraid poor Shay Broughton has had an accident. Jen phoned to let me know."

"Oh dear – is he badly hurt?"

"Well, it seems he was schooling his horse and they had some sort of accident. These things can happen so easily. He's in hospital but it's not too dire, just concussion and a few broken ribs."

"How dreadful. I'm sorry to hear it, but I expect it could have been worse."

Gary was upset about Shay, but pleased with the offer of a team place. He had tacked Moonrock so the girl mounted, with her black jacket in place, and set off to warm up gently. Her dressage test had improved so the score was higher than the previous time – and, it transpired, high enough to beat the other rider. She had qualified for Primary Dressage in the RDS.

Niall had found himself with free time at home and had taken himself off to the show before anyone could think of something that had to be done; he'd cycled to keep Tigger fresh for Sunday. Helping to calculate the dressage scores as they were handed in by the judge's assistant after each class, he heard about Shay's accident with dismay.

"We're still trying to form a second team for tomorrow," said the secretary. "Would you like to jump again? We were so pleased with your performance, and you'll be there for the individual class anyway. Without a top Open we're going to have to depend on the novices. The A team is going forward as it was last time."

"Sure, I'd love to," agreed Niall.

Karen arrived late. Jen had managed to contact anyone necessary and tell them of Shay's accident, so that the yard wasn't filled with young people expecting supervision, nor with buyers for young horses. Having cleared the decks, she had decided that they might as well go to the show. Karen had protested that she didn't mind missing the day, but Jen wanted to take their minds off the accident. By the time they got their horses plaited and groomed and drove to the show they were late. With less warming up than usual, Alabama performed a poor dressage test, not concentrating and avoiding the bit on the corners.

The equitation soon got under way and Karen snatched only a quick sandwich in order to spend plenty of time with her mare. Alabama responded well to the schooling and delivered her best ever round of equitation. Dirk rode well for Jen, enjoying himself. When the results were announced, Karen was placed second, only two points behind the winner, and Jen was third.

"Do you realise what this means?" Jen asked excitedly. "Since you had good scores all along, and Shay's out, you must have qualified."

"I can't have," breathed Karen, but sure enough Mrs Conroy came to ask Karen to represent the club in the RDS.

"And Jen," she added, "would you do the club a great favour? If you can manage to get away tomorrow, could you bring Karen and yourself to Clansha for a team?"

"Me?" Jen hadn't considered this possibility.

"I know you don't do much showjumping, and you've a young horse. But we are desperately short

of Opens. All you'd have to do is jump two rounds –
if you agree we can promote Karen to captain."

"Jen ought to be -" Karen began to protest, but
Jen stopped her.

"No, I've a very green horse. All right, but I don't
guarantee clear rounds as Dirk is still coming along
and this will be strange surroundings. I know how
important the Team Challenge is to everyone."

"That's wonderful." Mrs Conroy was beaming.
"Niall and Madeline are the novices."

Karen couldn't credit this development. Not only
picked for her second team, but captain…

The day's competitions having ended, Niall,
Madeline and Gary were planning strategy for the
morrow when Karen and Jen approached.

"Niall, have you transport?" asked Jen. "I could
arrange a lift for Tigger."

"I'm fine, thanks," replied Niall. "My father said
he'd come tomorrow and drive with the trailer, so
I'm okay."

"How did poor Shay's accident happen?" asked
Gary.

"He was schooling," described Jen. "The horse
spooked at a dry ditch under a fence and slipped
and fell with Shay underneath."

"We had to wait for the ambulance," added Karen.
"The men said that if we'd tried to move Shay, one
of his ribs might have punctured a lung. His temple
was bleeding but there was no damage there
except concussion, he was given an X-ray and CT
scan."

"He's awake now," Jen assured them. "His sister's travelling here today and we'll go in to the hospital before we go home for tea."

"Give him our best," said Gary, and the others concurred. "Was anyone else in the yard?"

"Some people had ridden out," answered Jen. "Karen and I were schooling a pony nearby but other than that he might have lain there for an hour or more."

"Just as well you were there," marvelled Madeline. "How about the horse?"

"Oh, he's okay," said Karen.

"Not a scratch," said Jen.

Shay sat upright in the bed, white sheets and bandages making his weathered skin ruddy and dark by contrast. Pillows propped him and a bandage covered the side of his head.

"Yes, of course it hurts," he answered Karen's tentative enquiry. "Every move of my arm pulls the muscles and every breath pushes out the ribcage. Apparently there's a nerve running along each rib, so broken ribs are sorer than most broken bones. But at least I didn't break my collarbone again."

"Everyone sent best wishes," Jen relayed. "Gary, the Conroys, Madeline, Niall, Hugh, Hannah, everyone."

"Everyone at the stables too," added Karen. "We saw your sister settled in to your house and she says she'll be in to see you again tonight."

"Hadn't seen Ann for more than a year," reflected Shay. "Christmas before last. So good of her to come."

"Family are for times of trouble," agreed Jen.

"And we'll take care of the yard until you're better," said Karen staunchly.

"Really? I expected Jen to say something about holiday time," said Shay innocently, and the girls laughed so much that the other patients gave quizzical stares. "But seriously, if Karen's putting in so many hours, Jen, we'll have to reduce her livery won't we?"

"She helps me with everything," the blonde girl agreed, smiling. "Well worth it. And we're organising the pony kids to clean tack and groom more often. They actually want to learn more – some of them."

"As for Cootehill Lad," directed Shay, "you can turn him out in a field. Don't either of you ride him."

"I didn't intend to," Jen assured him. "We didn't tell anyone exactly what happened, just as you asked."

"First offer I get, that horse goes, and without a warranty. Let some other dealer handle him. No reason why we should take risks like that, eh? He might just need a lot more schooling, but someone else can do it."

"That," declared Jen, "is the most sensible thing I've ever heard you say."

Shay shook his head sadly.

"I've just realised that I'm getting older," he sighed. "You go on and on just the same as always, until one day something like this hits you."

Madeline yawned as she went upstairs to bed.

"Goodnight, sweetheart," called her father.

"Are you sure you'll find your way tomorrow?" she asked anxiously. "A field won't be on the map on your phone."

"Yes, the directions were clear, and Gary says it'll be signposted."

"If in doubt," her mother considered, "we can probably follow a horsebox."

"I wish the day was over," the girl murmured to herself as she switched off her bedroom light and looked out at the moon. She wasn't dreading the event, on the contrary, she felt full of eager anticipation. But she wished she knew how the day would turn out … win or lose, just to know.

CHAPTER SIXTEEN

Niall rose at the crack of dawn to water and feed Tigger and his mother's old mare before getting on with the regular farm chores. His little brother Lorcan followed him excitedly and fetched brushes when Niall went back to groom Tigger. There was just about room for them all in the old calf shed where the pony lived. Lorcan chattered on about the show and having been to Mass on the previous evening. Saturday evening Mass was availed of by many these days.

"Can I brush him?"

"You can brush his tail," agreed Niall. "Like this, see?"

"Dad said he'd wash the car. He didn't want to arrive looking like he'd been driving through ditches."

"Just as long as he remembers we're loading Tigger and not a couple of bullocks...."

Jen and Karen had a lot of work on their hands. Every horse and pony had to be watered and fed, and each stable had to be cleaned out and hay distributed. The horses at grass had to be checked; the simplest way was by providing a small feed which drew them to the gate each morning. Cootehill Lad tried to bully the others away from their feeds and Jen made a note to ask Shay if they should call the blacksmith to remove the big gelding's hind shoes. While they were halfway through the yard routine, three young people turned up unexpectedly with offers of help. The girls gratefully accepted and the youngsters got to work.

Alabama and Dirk seemed not a whit tired and gobbled their feeds. Their plaits had stayed in place overnight and their coats gleamed when Karen took off the summer sheets they'd worn in the stables. When the two girls drove off with their horses, waving to Shay's sister Ann who'd provided strong tea, Karen felt excitement well up inside her from anticipation. Today, she felt, was going to be good. Her parents had expressed interest in coming to watch after she'd told them that not only was she to captain a team on the biggest day of the season, but she was to jump in the RDS that autumn. Naturally, she'd had to invite them. The girl wanted to mention her strongly positive feelings to Jen, but she had already discovered that horsey people were superstitious, and this might be regarded as a jinx.

"Isn't Ann lovely?" she said instead. "And to drop her own family at a moment's notice."

"She's being terrific," agreed Jen. "The children are teenagers though so it's not too bad."

"Why isn't Shay married?"

"I haven't a clue," returned Jen. "It's not the sort of question you'd ask anyone. Probably couldn't find a girl who would marry someone whose job depended on horses."

They laughed their way along the road, with the radio playing the latest news and music.

Clansha was based at a riding school, with members who seldom owned horses. Nearly all of the horses were stabled on the premises, which ensured a large turnout of the home crowd. The few horseboxes visible were therefore misleading. As always the individual competition was jumped first. Madeline had guessed that there must be only a few early entries but fifteen Primary riders competed. These riders were allowed to trot around the course if they wished, instead of taking a fair speed; the fences were barely two feet high and there were few faults. Madeline's parents arrived and stood watching proceedings, looking unimpressed.

"That's the class I started in," the girl admitted, only now realising her actual calibre. There were more entries in Intermediate.

"Is everyone who gets lessons here a club member?" puzzled Madeline as about the twelfth Clansha member entered the arena.

"Probably, for insurance reasons," agreed Gary, patting Moonrock's neck. "Concentrate on your course now – good luck."

Moonrock had to jump a fence of yellow and white poles with old tyres painted yellow and white underneath; a sheet of blue plastic holding water under a parallel; a wall painted to resemble a castle with stone-effect towers for wings; and a vertical of poles painted in spots instead of stripes.

After the artwork he'd been clearing at home nothing surprised him and he jumped faultlessly.

Nor did he make a mistake in the second round, so Madeline was cheered by her Dore Hill supporters. Clansha's president presented all eight double clear riders with a small red rosette and on the back of three were Xs; the rider drew rosettes from a hat and each lucky person got a small wooden shield. Madeline saw two being won, and almost screamed when there was an X on the back of her ribbon. Her first time to jump away from home ground, and she'd won an individual trophy.

The girl's parents swelled with pride, and Gary's beam threatened to split his head in two.

Niall, cheered by his entire family, jumped a double clear round and waited for the jump-off. Seven Advanced Intermediates were clear and he was drawn sixth. The Dore Hill contingent called support as he entered the arena with only two clears ahead of him. Tigger felt electrified and twisted as he jumped, shortening turns without effort. A long galloping distance to the last fence had already caught out most competitors, but Niall took a pull on the reins, knowing they had time. The pony responded to his schooling and steadied, getting his hocks under his body for a good jump over the parallel. An old hand, the blue water underneath had been scarcely a novelty to him. They flashed through the finish line clear.

"Watch this one," Gary warned as he met Niall at the pocket. "A hot-shot." The red roan mare entering the arena had been jumping big and fast, switching her black tail madly over every obstacle. About fifteen-two hands, she was nippy but longer-legged than the pony.

"I don't know her," said Niall.

"Grade D jumper," Gary told him. "I remember her well. She retired when she got to a grade she couldn't cope with."

"Red Minnow with Tracy Larkin for Clansha Riding Club," called the announcer. The roan, clipping back her ears, shot around the course, her rider kicking flat-out and guiding the turns. She took time off Niall's last gallop with her longer stride and stood off from the last fence, soaring across and landing galloping. She cut half a second off Niall's time.

"We'll give the lass a clap then," the farmer told his sons equably.

Karen and Jen walked the Open course, which appeared formidable.

"Alabama's never jumped water," moaned Karen.

"Kick on hard so she hasn't time to see it," Jen advised. "I didn't intend to jump in the individual event but Dirk must see that gaudy course or he'll go bananas in the team event. He's only done rustics and a few coloured poles – what is he going to make of it all?"

Dirk was decidedly put out and cat-jumped over several fences, a horrified expression on his honest face, dragging poles as he forgot his lessons. Less generous novices might have refused. He incurred twelve faults, which Jen told the Dore Hill people she was considering as just a practise round.

Alabama's eyes practically stood out on stalks and Karen wished she'd been permitted to walk the mare around the arena while she inspected the course. Remembering Jen's advice, she tapped the mare's shoulder with her whip about two strides before each fence, and kicked on hard to anything awkward. The mare cleared the spooky fences strongly. Karen found riding smoothly was difficult, and in the second round they met a tall vertical of a pole over fertiliser bags on an impossible stride. Alabama tried to shorten, managed a half-stride but just pushed the top pole off its cup.

"Hard luck," Mrs Conroy consoled her. "Keep her fresh now, for the team event."

"She was jumping better that time than the first," said Karen.

"We appreciate that she's still green," said the secretary.

There were two Advanced Open riders, who enjoyed a fast and furious speed round. Then a break for lunch was announced, and the course was adjusted so everyone could walk it during the interval.

When the novice level commenced for the team event, Niall volunteered to go first for his team and the others agreed. Tigger was getting to know the fences by now and pulled on the bit but scrambled over everything. Madeline took a steadying breath and resolved to try her hardest. Moonrock felt keen as ever and never came close to hitting anything. The girl she'd met from Clansha previously, Niamh, was mounted on a better horse today and collected just four faults; they exchanged smiles.

Jen was next to jump for the team and took Dirk around at a steady pace, allowing him to size up the unfamiliar obstacles. The iron grey knew that he'd got over these fences already and just shied at the white timing apparatus at start and finish. He collected eight faults but had improved.

"Up to you," sighed Jen to Karen.

Gary constructed practise fences as Madeline held Moonrock in shade and sipped a fizzy drink. Alabama cantered smoothly, as though she was doing an equitation round. Karen felt confident despite the pressure from Jen's faults, and rode with extra care. The mare knew the fences by now and gave them just enough space, not wasting energy.

"Wonderful!" shrieked Madeline as Karen went clear. The team was clear overall, and only three other teams were also clear, including their own A team.

"What does that mean?" asked her father diffidently, so she had to explain the situation. Eamonn listened with seeming concentration.

"The home club is short on Opens," added Gary. "One of their teams has three novices. They can work that way around but not three Opens or they'd have an advantage."

Trotting Moonrock around the practise arena again, Madeline felt relieved to be away from people. Her mount had done a lot of work yesterday and today; would he be fit enough? She'd given him a small drink, just a couple of mouthfuls. She halted to watch Niall who set off on his second round with care and steadied Tigger frequently. The dun pony rode obediently, getting tired in the heat.

Niall went clear – much to his relief. He emerged and jumped off Tigger, who was immediately fed mints by the Johnson brothers.

"Tigger is the bestest," declared the partisan young Lorcan.

"You know what, Lorcan, I'm growing again," Niall told his little brother, showing that his cuff was up his wrist. "I'll be too big for Tigger soon, and then you can ride him."

The next rider collected seven faults and then Madeline's turn came. The grey horse started gamely but began to feel tired and barely cleared his fences. The girl knew he was doing his best and concentrated on helping him as much as possible. Moonrock jumped the second last fence sparingly and his short landing altered the related distance to the parallel with water. Realising that they were somehow meeting the last fence wrongly, the girl sat firm, pushed and assisted with her hands. Moonrock made a valiant effort, took off on a long stride and gained his height – but couldn't make the distance and came down on the back bar with his hind fetlocks. The pole bounced and instead of dropping back into the cup, fell for four faults. Madeline rode out, patting her game little cob, hanging her head with dejection.

"That was tough," said her father in commiseration. "Isn't he a great jumper though? Really tried."

"We're still in with a chance," Gary consoled her.

Madeline untacked Moonrock and gave him a little more tepid water. Everyone else was keeping track of matters at the ringside; Dore Hill A's novice Sinead also incurred four faults. Maybe it wasn't too bad, Madeline dared to hope. The team might still gain a placing.

Dirk pricked up his dark ears and studied each fence, picking up his feet intelligently. He not only knew the arena now, he knew the course, and Jen, riding as though her life depended on a clear, kept expecting to hear a pole fall right until they crossed the finish line. She was so proud of her green horse that she fed him pieces of apple immediately they left the arena, without even taking off his bridle; he chewed and slobbered and jingled the bit, pleased with himself.

"That's a fine looking girl," Jamie told his younger brother Niall. "Why have I not seen her jumping at these big shows before? I'd have noticed, I like blonde girls. What's her name?"

"Never mind her, look at the gorgeous redhead on the chestnut," breathed Sean.

"I hate to tell you Karen," groaned Mrs Conroy, "but it all depends on you."

Tight-lipped, Karen secured her girth and saddle check and gave Alabama the minimum of preparation, so as not to tire her.

"Doesn't she look beautiful," marvelled Mrs Langourne. "Did her groom do all that plaiting this morning?"

"Actually," responded her daughter, "I did that myself. I'm a horsewoman, not just a rider."

The Langournes, glancing at each other, stepped up to the ropes to watch. The mare was so fit that she had plenty of energy and never looked like faltering. She tried her best to please, jumping with a classic style.

"That's our daughter," pointed out Mrs Langourne to a distinguished-looking gentleman beside her, adding, "She's an excellent horsewoman; she's won several prizes with the mare already."

"Karen? Lovely girl," agreed Hugh Roe. "I, er, don't recall her mentioning it." He introduced himself politely, adding that he was from Karen's club, and her parents exchanged names happily.

"That handsome shield in front of the judges, is that the prize? If Karen's team wins, will she be able to keep it? She is the captain after all." Mrs Langourne could see that shield on the mantelpiece already. She might give a small cocktail party. Which ladies would she invite? she mused.

"I really couldn't say," murmured Hugh.

"Clear round for Alabama putting Dore Hill B into a good spot; double clear round total."

"Anyone else?" Karen asked generally as she dismounted and loosened girths.

"Most teams have a small amount of faults," answered Mrs Conroy. "Our A team still has a good chance – four faults this round but Fiona has yet to go. Home team A has done well so it looks like a jump-off."

In the event a jump-off was announced between four teams – a measure of the extremely high standard that day. The home team Clansha A got drawn first, then Dore Hill A, Dore Hill B and Rathcarn. The home club's Open rider was mounted on a steady riding-school type of horse, which picked up his knees with reliable agility but liked to trot around corners. He delivered a steady clear.

Fiona Conroy threw her heart into her round, cut corners and blazed a gallop to the final fence on this shortened course, a plank. But her good little horse, though willing, was tired and just tapped her knees off the top plank, flattening with speed. Down crashed the plank for four faults.

"Whew," breathed Karen, who had known that she couldn't have hoped to beat Fiona's spectacular round – up to that point. Alabama felt sharp and excited under her, and the merest tap of the whip against her shoulder was sufficient to set her jogging.

"Go clear," ordered Gary, and Jen affirmed this decision. Better not take any stupid risks, decided Karen. There was a turn Fiona had made though – after a fence she'd gone between the elements of the double instead of around them. The bell rang and they were off at a smart canter, making sure to clear the first fence and counting off the altered track. Alabama made a sharp dodge right when asked and cut between the elements of the double, ears pricked as Karen sighted the next jump and steered. The chestnut was excited and gained speed as she went, so that Karen didn't know whether to check for the final fence and risk putting her off her stride, or gallop to it the way Fiona had. With the plank fast approaching, she sat straight as if to ride dressage, in order to keep the mare's forehand off the ground. At a long stride she asked with hands, legs and voice for a big jump and the mare rose for a tremendous arc, clearing the plank well and landing far out beyond the fence.

"Clear in a good time," she heard as she rode out, clapping the mare's shoulder and laughing. All her team-mates and club members set up a rousing cheer, for she had well beaten the home side. The final rider came in for his turn. Taking up the challenge, he attempted a sharp turn before the double. However he met it on a half stride and his horse hesitated, jumped and paddled in the air, sending poles crashing and putting them wrong for the second element, which also fell. He finished to sympathetic applause.

"So the winners are Dore Hill B," the judge announced. Karen shrieked with delight, to the surprise of her parents, who had thought her such a quiet child.

Madeline, Niall, Jen and Karen had to remount hastily, waving to supporters and tugging girths, for a parade in the arena. The other teams lined up behind them, with much laughter and handshaking from team to team. Each horse on the winning team had a red sash draped around its neck. The riders were presented with many-tiered red and white rosettes, trailing long gold-lettered tails. Each of them received a small wooden memento trophy while the large wooden Regional Shield, with spaces for inscriptions on the silver front plate, was presented to the team captain.

"I do wish she'd look this way," grumbled Mrs Langourne, aiming her camera. "Karen!" She managed to get some pleasing shots.

Karen clutched the trophy tightly, glad she'd left her whip outside, and when all prizes had been awarded Karen led them in a lap of honour. The teams cantered proudly around the arena to tremendous applause. Jen had told Karen that horses loved this, and the girl could feel that she had been correct. Alabama gave a little skip and squeal of joy.

Outside, dismounting, the team admired the wonderful shield.

"We hold it for three months each and return it next year," Jen explained to the others.

"In that case," Karen said promptly, "I reckon the most junior member ought to hold it first." She presented the shield to Madeline, much to that girl's astonishment.

"Agreed," said Niall. "Madeline and Moonrock were fantastic."

Jen laughed and nodded.

Mrs Langourne's eyes glittered with envy as she saw her daughter part with the magnificent shield; Karen caught her father's eye, and he was glowing with pride.

"That's my girl," he said, as he gave Karen a kiss on the cheek.

"These pictures are getting tweeted right now," Niall's brothers were assuring him. "Your luck to get on a team with the three best-looking girls in the county."

"Yeah, you're right there," Niall stated. "Not just looks either. The three finest young ladies you could meet. Madeline, Karen, Jen, we have to celebrate. There's a harvest dance at the hotel next Friday; would you be up for that? I mean, with boyfriends if you want to bring someone, or if not, myself and my brothers Sean and Jamie would be delighted to take you. Anyone over sixteen can go. We can get the tickets." They weren't actually refusing. Emboldened, the lad continued. "There's a band before a buffet supper and then a disco, you can e-mail requests in advance so there'll be all kinds of music. All kinds," he repeated, willing Madeline to

158

accept. This girl had sincerely impressed him as a team-mate.

"Sounds great, Madeline, you should go as a reward," the girl's mother agreed when Madeline looked at her for permission.

"Karen, I'm certainly not going to turn down a good offer from such fine young men," said Jen, winking, because the harvest dances were legendary entertainment.

"I'd love to go, thanks very much, Niall," said Karen, "and I'd be pleased to go with you and your brothers. We can all turn up as a team."

"I'm Sean, and this is Jamie," spoke up Sean immediately, and they all shook hands.

"This win should do our chance of getting Lottery funding some good," said Mrs Conroy happily to her husband as they snapped final photos.

"The event and win have done some good already, looks like," he replied with a smile.

THE END

RODEO FINN

By Clare O'Beara

Finn Dwyer, aged fifteen, is growing up on a dairy farm in Ireland, her thoughts of horses and friendships. When she is challenged in the worst way, she doesn't know how to go forward in life.

Summer on her uncle's ranch in Arizona with her cousin Sean and a beautiful black mare Juana gives Finn the chance to let go of her unhappiness. Not only does she explore the Sonora Desert, she learns trail riding, cattle roping and rodeo skills.

When her strength and decisiveness are called upon however, will Finn prove herself?

Another atmospheric story of young adults, horses and challenges from the author of
SHOW JUMPING TEAM.

The Prisoner In The Tower

& Big Cat Bones

Short Story

By Clare O'Beara

Aged ten, Nat is lucky enough to come to work in the Tower of London. King Edward is fighting France, but his household needs staff. The Tower contains prisoners - and a menagerie, including the King's Lion.

Big Cat Bones is the background to this tale, explaining the forensic archaeology which has discovered fascinating historical details about lynx and lion in England.

DINING OUT AROUND THE SOLAR SYSTEM

by Clare O'Beara

JUPITER'S BOUGHT THE DOME!

Donal, an Irish lad, and Myron, a Cockney-Jamaican mix, meet aged seventeen as book reviewers and trainee journalists. Before long they're onto the hottest stories in London.

DEATH CAUSED BY CAFFEINE

In their future, Stansted Airport has been converted to a space shuttle base and Londoners are recruited to mine the asteroids.

AHOY NEPTUNE! ESTUARY BOMBS TO BE CLEARED

While exploring the other planets, we found that they were all inhabited. Now those people are coming to Earth and looking for work. They're also opening ethnic restaurants in central London.

THE SMOKING GUN

Befriending immigrants makes Donal and Myron unpopular with some, while their investigative reporting lands them in trouble with wealthy organisations, criminals and the Home Office. Their romantic prospects are compromised. But you can't keep a good team down, especially when they report for *London's Eye,* and they've got every book ever digitised at their disposal....

STOWAWAYS FROM SATURN

Excerpt from

Dining Out Around The Solar System

Book One in the *Dining Out Around The Solar System* series.

"You should know that." Pietr sounded serious. "You guys find a great story like this in some different zine, it gets taken away from you and handed to me. You might get your names as researchers on the bottom. You find this story as a freelancer, what do you think happens?"

"We sell it?" Myron asked.

"You go to jail," said Pietr.

A RIB is a rigid inflatable boat, and this has an engine at the rear which pushes the nose up and out of the water as it bounces along at a great speed. This was a good-sized one and I realised that it must have an antigrav component because it never sank in the water though the team of Neptunians got on with us. The marine engineer steering it took us out to the dive boat, a large – to our eyes – vessel over a mile offshore. We sat back and gripped the rope lacings along the sides and breathed in salt spray air, grinning foolishly at our friends and each other. The RIB engine was so noisy that we couldn't really talk but we were relishing being right down at water level, streaking across the Thames estuary, heading for the most dangerous boat in the world.

MURDER AT IRISH MENSA

by Clare O'Beara

Cara Cassidy, a Dublin tree surgeon, is having a tough May weekend. Her landlady has given her notice. Cara's in the middle of organising an international convention for the high intelligence group Irish Mensa. Visiting tobacco heiress Laurel Cabot – who has married a Dubliner with the paper title of Baron of Ballymun – is murdered and her priceless diamond necklace stolen. Both the Gardai and Interpol believe that the killer is among the guests.

Amid visits to the National Stud and Trinity College, Cara – newly elected Chairman of Irish Mensa - does some investigating, with the aid of Mike Fraser, a Scottish guest. The Mensa members trust her, but some people would prefer their secrets to remain hidden....

MURDER AT SCOTTISH MENSA

by Clare O'Beara

Cara Cassidy and Mike Fraser, newly a couple, are visiting a Scottish Mensa Weekend held in Stirling in July, complete with a medieval costume banquet at the Castle. Cara is assaulted by Danny Dreffin, an unemployed, unpopular Glaswegian computer programmer who is trying to get her into bed. Mike has a public row with this man, a Scottish Nationalist, and has no alibi when the Glaswegian is later found beaten to death.

Central Scotland Police believe Mike may be the killer and Cara turns to a Mensan Garda detective in Dublin, Ricky Norton, for help. He agrees to work on the case if they send him information by e-mail about their fellow Mensan guests. Then it seems that everyone is pleased that Dreffin is dead. Asking questions of the guests from various countries is certain to put the couple in danger, and they only have one day to keep Mike from being charged.

MURDER AT KILDARE MENSA

by Clare O'Beara

Retired businessman Thomas McGlone is shot dead during a break-in at his home in Co. Kildare, when several thousand euro he'd just won by betting on racing is stolen. His son Tiernan, a member of the high IQ group Mensa, who works for a firm of stockbrokers, is implicated. This man, his sister and brother-in-law from London have lost their savings in the financial crash.

Cara Cassidy, a former showjumper and Chairman of Irish Mensa, agrees to help the family get the deceased man's racehorse mares to stud. Ricky Norton, her Garda detective friend, forbids her to investigate the death but is covering the case himself, to the displeasure of the Kildare police.

Cara's boyfriend Mike Fraser is running a parachuting event in nearby Clonbullogue and Cara plans to make a charity skydive. But she's in far more danger on the ground....

Adult Romantic Suspense

from Clare O'Beara

SILKS AND SINS

Geri and Jackie O'Keane inherit their father's riding stables in Ireland and, both business women, set about modernising, including a website. When Jackie meets Valentine Murney, a rising star in the flat racing world, her life appears complete. Val, who admits that he's no saint, is dedicated, good looking, kind, and a great lover. Jackie sets her sights on the highly competitive 'most stylish lady' raceday prizes. Meanwhile Geri is drifting towards her own relationship.

But when two spiteful stable girls tell Jackie that her jockey boyfriend has been sleeping with someone else, she faces making a decision which might be the greatest mistake of her life.

About The Author

Clare O'Beara is a tree surgeon and expert witness, and a former national standard showjumper.
She has been elected Chairman of Irish Mensa and Director of British Mensa Ltd. She was also appointed National Representative to Mensa International.
She serves on the Royal Dublin Society Forestry Awards Committee.
She lives in Dublin with her husband and cats.

Clare is an award-winning writer of fiction and non-fiction, whose journalism work has been published in more than thirty countries. Her credits include *Mensa Magazine* and *Mensa International Journal*.
In 2013 she won first prize for Print Journalism in Ireland's National Media Awards.
In 2014 she won the Arkady Renko Short Story Contest, judged by Martin Cruz Smith, with *London Calling*.
She contributed a story to *A Pint And A Haircut* (Lon Dubh, 2010), an anthology in aid of Concern's Haiti fund.
Clare reads extensively and reviews books for Fresh Fiction.com.

Check out her books on
http://www.clareobeara.ie

FREE READ of Clare's 2014 award-winning crime short story

London Calling on the Simon and Schuster website:

http://the-dark-pages-blog.blogspot.i...

Meet Clare on Goodreads.

https://www.goodreads.com

Science Fiction

Dining Out Around The Solar System
Dining Out With The Ice Giants
Dining Out With The Gas Giants

Crime

Murder at Irish Mensa
Murder at Scottish Mensa
Murder at Dublin Mensa
Murder at Kildare Mensa
Murder at Wicklow Mensa

Romantic Suspense

Silks And Sins

Young Adult

Show Jumping Team
Rodeo Finn

Short Story

The Prisoner In The Tower

Anthologies

Dreamless Roads

A Pint And A Haircut

If you have enjoyed this book, please consider leaving a review on Amazon and Goodreads to help other readers. Your time is much appreciated.

Printed in Great Britain
by Amazon

85243424R00102